ALCATRAZ AWAITS:
THE LEGACY OF DONALD TRUMP

ALCATRAZ AWAITS:
THE LEGACY OF DONALD TRUMP

John H. Cary

Copyright © 2024 John H. Cary. All rights reserved.

No part of this book may be reproduced or transmitted in any form or by any means, graphic, electronic, or mechanical, including photocopying, recording, taping, or by any information storage retrieval system, without the permission, in writing, of the publisher. For more information, send an email to support@sbpra.net, Attention: Subsidiary Rights.

Strategic Book Publishing
www.sbpra.net

For information about special discounts for bulk purchases, please contact Strategic Book Publishing, Special Sales, at bookorder@sbpra.net.

ISBN: 978-1-63410-161-5

Contents

Part 1 1
    Chapter 1 3
    Chapter 2 10
    Chapter 3 15
    Chapter 4 20
    Chapter 5 28
    Chapter 6 36
    Chapter 7 41
    Chapter 8 44
    Chapter 9 54

Part 2 61
    Chapter 1 63
    Chapter 2 79
    Chapter 3 83
    Chapter 4 89
    Chapter 5 94
    Chapter 6 98

Part 3 103
Chapter 1 105
Chapter 2 118
Chapter 3 124

Part 4 131
Chapter 1 133
Chapter 2 138
Chapter 3 142
Chapter 4 148
Chapter 5 156
Chapter 6 169
Chapter 7 174
Chapter 8 181

Chapter I

"Donald John Trump, for crimes against the people and the state, you are hereby found guilty. Do you have any final words to say before sentence is carried out?"

"That's President Donald John Trump to you..."

"That title no longer exists. You *will* be remembered as the forty-fifth president of the United States but from this point forward you will only be known as an inmate with a number which should be easy to remember and something you should be proud of, prisoner number zero four five or Inmate 045. You may continue."

"I have a wife and teenage son!" Trump began to shout.

"You had. You had a wife and teenage son. As of earlier this morning, she divorced you and by the way, a recent DNA test confirmed the child is not even yours. What do you think of them apples?"

"Divorced me? I didn't agree to it."

"Is this your signature?"

"Uh yeah."

"While in this courtroom, you will address me as Your Honor."

"Okay, your honor," came the sarcastic remark, "yes, that is my signature. It has to be a fake like the news and election and this trial, this kangaroo court. The kid's not mine? No surprise. I've probably got a bunch of them floating around myself."

"We have witnesses and videos. Your ex-wife had you sign it. See? Look at the monitor."

"That sneaky bitch!"

"Guess you were too busy pardoning people at the last minute of your presidency that you didn't notice. Next time, oh there won't be a next time, you had best read things before you sign them," one of the judges remarked with a grin.

"As I was saying or about to say, this entire court, this entire trial is rigged. It's a fraud, just like the election. I am the president and will return as president! I will always be the president! I'm the most popular president in the history of the world. I have a billion loyal subjects. I won the election by four hundred million votes! God voted for me, absentee of course but he voted for me. I have billions of dollars. Putting me in prison will cost the tax payers millions…"

This continued for the next three hours until finally the judges had endured enough finally asking the bailiff to gag the former president and force him to be seated and restrained. Several of the judges had fallen asleep along with most of the small audience.

"It was bad enough hearing you rant and rave for four years but in this enclosed space it was even worse. Getting back to sanity, the court sentences you to spend the rest of your life, natural or otherwise on the former United States penitentiary known as Alcatraz which has been closed due to the pandemic and will not be reopened despite its popularity. However, people will be allowed to come within a specified distance with the hopes of catching a glimpse of you. Kind like whale watching. Tickets are sold out for years. One billion dollars of your own money has been set aside for your maintenance and upkeep which means there will be no guards to watch you. There will be no staff on the island yet you will be monitored. Bi-monthly food deliveries will be flown in by helicopter and twice a week you will have meals sent to you by drones. Under strict orders, no personnel is to communicate with or to you in any form. You will not be allowed mail, phone calls or anything. In other words you will be completely alone and for the most part cut off from the outside world. A fund has been established by your supporters to continue your upkeep even though half will go to your former wife. She is even selling t-shirts with your image and name with you holding the bars on your cell or standing on a hill preaching to sheep and other animals. I actually bought one. You will have access to internet and television but you will not be allowed any contact with the outside world. There will be no communication which means you will not be able send or receive any messages. Any attempts of a rescue or your escape will be dealt with in severe manners. In other words, Mr. Trump, that is Inmate 045, if anyone tries to fly in or access you in any other fashion, they will be blown away by automated defenses. If you look at the monitor, you will see how it was recently tested. Tour boats will be informed of the same thing and there will be patrols. Welcome to exile Inmate 045. Reminds you of Napoleon, doesn't it? Consider yourself lucky. Execution was being considered by firing squad since you have also been charged and convicted with sedition and treason. Unlike you, we had something called evidence."

    On the screen to the left of the judges, a video was displayed in which a small remote controlled plane was shown attempting to breach the airspace of the island and it was completely destroyed as was a small boat which tried to come within the distance equivalent of three football fields. An unmanned helicopter met the same fate. This was broadcast on the worldwide web and all major networks covering the short trial. Even though the former chief executive was by law allowed legal counsel, nobody would represent him as the evidence was overwhelming. Several of his other lawyers had already made plea bargains to testify against their former friend and boss in exchange for immunity or reduced sentences yet since by law an attorney had to be appointed, the one who had met with him earlier and explained he had no case.

"Sir, I have been practicing law for twenty years and have never seen so much evidence against one client in my entire career. You are a case for textbooks and are lucky they didn't take you out and shoot you. All I can do is what the court orders as you are legally bound to be represented by an attorney. You would have a better chance of representing yourself. The only reason you have me is because I made a deal that my name or image would never be displayed. I will probably write a book about the case but aside from that, it's an embarrassment to represent you," said the bald African American as they sat together the week before discussing the upcoming proceedings.

"As you can see Mr. Trump there is no one that can come to you. Your wife now former wife who has filed for a petition of divorce which has been granted has been given that money plus custody of half of all your assets which means in some ways you are a free man. You will be taken to the island known as Alcatraz the day after tomorrow because the first thing in the morning, you will have full day of orientation to prison life yet you will not have to worry about being harmed by other inmates because you will be the only one there. On the island you will also have access to fishing and hunting as small game such as rabbits were transplanted several months ago along with a small herd of goats and sheep. You will have access to archery equipment and traps. Good luck. This case is closed. Next!"

"What about the library? My fucking Donald Trump Presidential Library!" he shouted as the gag was removed while he wiped the saliva with his sleeve.

"Plenty of room for it where you will be going. Take your book, THE ART OF THE DEAL. The former prison library has lots of other books that still remain from back in the day. If you need to learn something like how to cook rabbit, shear, milk or cook sheep or goats, you can google it," the judges snickered as the prisoner was escorted out.

"When I return, I will find and have you all hanged. I am the President of the United States! God save the queen! I mean I shall return!" he continued to yell thrusting his forefinger into the air in defiance.

It was a rapid trial and the evidence had been accumulating for years practically from the first day the forty-fifth president of the United States of America took office and even before. Some others had been put on hold such as tax evasion which turned out to be one of the items that had brought Donald Trump down just as it did the former mob boss Al "Scarface" Capone. He had even attempted to impose Martial Law to get the military to overturn the election which lead to the charges of treason plus the fact that he had to be forcibly evicted from the White House by the United States Secret Service. The punishment had been a tough decision for the judges and there was some sympathy for the former president. Had he been a private citizen or one without the notoriety, it would have been a simple matter of giving him x amount of years and that would have been the end of it but this was different. Of course, as mentioned, execution was on the table and would have happened if he had not been Donald John Trump. He had to be put away to where he could not create mischief but having him in a prison environment would have been a security nightmare so the idea of using the former maximum security prison known affectionately as "The Rock" was the best alternative. By law any former president was to be provided with Secret Service protection for the rest of their lives but a quick constitutional amendment was ratified at which any former president with a felony conviction was not allowed such privilege. The attack on the Capitol Building was found to be his doings and from his orders as there were written statements verifying everything. Then came the time when he stole classified documents claiming they were his and began to brag about them and show them around to others which was what really did him in. On the island, there would be no guards, administrative or support staff. Inmate 045 would be responsible for his own meals aside from the ones delivered by drone once a week as well as washing his own clothes and dishes. None of these were required. The prison was self-sufficient as far as water and power due to solar and wind so he was to be a very cheap convict. In fact, he cost the tax payers nothing except for some contractors who had come in to update the kitchen and a few other areas about a week before. Money that had been taken from him was to be paid to the other contractors and employees he had cheated over the years in his various businesses which were all sold.

Donald Trump's former wife, the former first lady could have been a problem yet was an easy remedy due to her own suggestions. It was agreed upon that even though she was given one billion dollars from her husband's estate, she was also to be given a small stipend which came to more than most middle class families make in a year and this money was to come from the fund in which her ex-husband had from his still loyal followers. She and her son decided to have cosmetic surgery and their identities altered and placed in the Witness Protection Program in a small college town somewhere in the Pacific Northwest so with their altered identities and appearances plus her change in voice which was enhanced by some minor surgery on her vocal cords, they would remain unnoticed and soon forgotten. Her husband had embarrassed her and there were times when people felt she was the same as he was whereas nothing could be any more wrong. Often, she laid awake in bed at night wondering why she had ever married the man. She knew it wasn't for his money so finally she attributed it to his charisma and her own immaturity and let it go at that. The marriage had long been over but the main thing was that she loved her son and nothing could change that. She had even loved the child's father even though briefly and in a fit of passion that lasted a few months and during periods of loneliness and sexual frustration. With Donald safely out of the way, she could begin to live a simple life, perhaps one in which she could have a small house with a garden and even a dog and no more being constantly watched and critiqued and hounded by the press.

Chapter 2

The people were tired of Donald J. Trump, President Trump. They were tired of his thin skin, daily rants, lies, uncaring attitude and conspiracy theories. Oh he did care about one thing and that was himself. He probably kissed himself in the mirror every morning. For four years America and the world had endured him but there were those who loved him while believing every single word that came out of his constantly moving mouth. He was elected because he was different. He was rude, brash and a businessman. Being a man of business and a multibillionaire on top of that, people just assumed he would be the one to run the country. Many did not trust his opponent yet there were also those who did not necessarily like him at the time so they did what is common in America and that is to choose the lesser of two evils. With his insults during the election such as threatening to lock up his opponent and to charge Mexico for a wall he planned to build, his followers mistook bullying for courage. Donald Trump was unaware of the workings of the United States government and politics in general as he must have believed that to be president and if he wished something, all he had to do was sign a paper or give an order and it would be done instantly. He was gravely mistaken that a United States president was limited in his powers yet had the idea that it was like a king or CEO and felt that those in Congress were mere figureheads pretending to represent the people. The wall with Mexico for example was not as simple as it sounded. It was to be a massive undertaking not only with men and equipment along with planning and materials but having to purchase land from the owners on which it was to be constructed but this was just a small thing and a promise eventually he realized could not be kept, a promise one of many.

It didn't take long before his constant need for stroking his ego grew tiresome along with the daily insults of members of Congress, world leaders and anyone who offended or disagreed with him. People expected him to be more presidential as had his predecessor but instead, he almost immediately began campaigning for a second term. He had been a reality show host and had to always be in the spotlight. His name or the Trump name was everywhere. There was the Trump Towers, Trump Hotels, casinos, resorts, golf courses and on and on. People put up with his blatant disregard for kindness and tact plus the fact that he had no filters as to what he said and it was as if his mouth moved before his brain was used.

Donald Trump was a showman. His insecurities had to be constantly fed yet he also had to be pampered and surrounded himself with yes men who, for the most part were appointed not because of their qualifications but due to how well they stroked his already inflated ego. The minute someone disagreed with him, they were either publicly admonished or fired with little warning and then he was never satisfied so he would frequently attack them some even after they were long dead. If he hated someone he hated them all the way to the grave often not attending to or being invited to funerals or honoring soldiers who had lost their lives defending the country even to the point of insulting a father's military son who had been killed in action while visiting his grave. He had spent years challenging the birth location of the former president, a kind man of great intelligence which obviously intimidated him. Some of his cabinet members were hardened military with decades of experience on and off the battlefield yet when they even made a slight comment asking the president to alter a course of action, they were gone. It was a revolving door regarding appointments. The president had knowledge of business but very little in regard to politics and the law and was under the impression that he was the supreme leader holding as much or more power as those who ran countries such as Russia, China or North Korea. If Donald Trump didn't like someone including a previous president, every item including portraits were placed in a room out of the way almost a storage area where they could not be seen especially by himself. His own staff began to fear his temper tantrums and for at least the second half of his term, walked on eggshells to avoid upsetting him and bringing out his wrath.

When the pandemic came to American shores beginning as an outbreak from some mutated virus which originated at a wet market in China, this was to test what kind of leader he was in a crisis. He failed or at least in a few ways. Sure, he initially shut done the flights from China and a few other nations but by then it was too late but then he reversed course by ignoring the directives of medical advisors such as the wearing of masks and social distancing. He even made it a point to insult the Chinese repeatedly by calling the virus the China virus instead of what the scientists and doctors were calling it. A good leader leads by example; Trump did not. Often at odds with the top virologists in the country if not the world, as he tried to take credit for doing one thing right while failing with others. A smart person doesn't have to tell others of their high intelligence because people can tell. Donald Trump, however was always telling of how smart and great and of his accomplishments even to the point of announcing that he was smarter than anyone he had ever known. What kind of person does that? It was always "me, me, me." He was a classic case of Imposter Phenomenon plus a host of others. As the experts were telling him one thing such as to wear a mask, he was rarely if ever seen with one and when told that Americans needed to have limited and small gatherings, he continued to hold massive rallies to feed his unquenchable ego or holding what was called super spreaders which only increased the cases and deaths. He did expedite the development of vaccines yet when the election came and he lost in the popular and electoral vote and numbers the pandemic was basically forgotten as he went on continual rants filing useless lawsuits without any evidence hiring his friends who happened to be attorneys yet with limited knowledge and mostly years of lives in politics. His bullying tactics began to wear on everyone and got to where he threatened at least one state governor with imprisonment if he did not change or alter the election in his favor. Americans continued to die while he ignored them spending most of his time sending out negative messages on social media and time on the golf course. It had become apparent that he wasn't as successful as he had claimed having filed for bankruptcy numerous times and gaining his money by either underpaying or not paying workers and contractors at all. His refusal to turn over his tax returns was part of his undoing as they eventually showed massive contradictions and fraud. The election was not rigged. Trump lost because of Trump but he had proven that he wasn't even a success at losing. Obviously, the final straw or one of them was when overwhelming evidence pointed out that he was the one who planned and tried to have the election overturned but his vice president at the time stood his ground and followed the law of the land despite a hoard of fanatical minions attacking what was supposed to be a peaceful transfer of power. Then came the even more damning evidence of those classified documents thus labeling him as a traitor.

Yes, people were tired of Donald John Trump. When he became a private citizen without the protection he had as president, the lawsuits and subpoenas came in mass. Often talking with his lawyer friends, they had already begun to distance themselves as they realized that despite the pardons they had received earlier, they were not immune to prosecution on the state levels even though were so against federal charges. When he had told people earlier in his presidency that he could walk out in the middle of New York City and shoot someone dead and nobody could do a thing showing how powerful he was, this was one comment that came back to haunt him. Therefore, as soon as the next president was officially sworn in becoming the forty-six president in American history, Donald Trump came to the realization that he was a doomed man.

Chapter 3

It was a small holding cell with one bed, one sink and toilet with no other prisoners in the entire building. His handcuffs were removed, was fed a simple meal without complaint and promptly at nine o'clock was given a sedative which went to work within minutes and he was fast asleep. At 6:00 the following morning he was awakened in a neutral manner, allowed to shower and prepare and dress as he pleased not in standard prison garb but in his usual custom-made tailored suit, given breakfast and then precisely at 8:00 taken into a room for orientation.

"This is your introduction to your new home, the Island of Alcatraz where you will spend the rest of your life," the middle aged somewhat attractive brunette began. "If you have any questions during this briefing, you only have to ask. A notebook and pens have been provided for you."

"Yeah, I have a question. Where's my wallet? I had a hell of a lot of cash in there along with credit cards. I'm a rich man," the former president began.

"Sir, where you're going, there are no stores so you may be rest assured that for the rest of your life you will never spend one cent ever again and as far as identification is concerned, you don't even have a name anymore. You are simply a number. Your wallet and other former forms of identification will be placed in section devoted to former presidents for tourists to see at the White House. I do believe there is a picture of Alcatraz with a caption that tells where you are living. Last night a device was surgically implanted into your neck next to a major blood vessel where it cannot be removed safely. This will monitor your vitals which will be constantly transmitted to a central computer base. Other than that you are on your own. Personally, nobody cares where you are or go on the island but we do not advise you to venture into the water because it's very cold and sharks abound. There also mines so of the three, certainly one or more will get you. The next presenter will more than likely mention these again."

"I took a tour of Alcatraz years ago and they said there is no natural water supply and that when it was a prison, they had to bring in a million gallons a week."

"That is true but recently a state of the art water filtration plant was built which extracts salt and impurities from sea water and purifies it making it as clean as the water in the bottle in front of you. The plant runs itself but is monitored constantly from an office on the mainland so if there is any sort of problem, a team of technicians will be sent in to correct it. Actually, there are two of these so if one goes down, the second starts up and they are guaranteed to outlive you especially in light of your weight, former eating and exercise habits and the like. Also you might see some windmills which not only provide power but also extract water from the air which is sent to holding tanks. You will never run out of water or power. Besides, the million gallons a week was for a lot more than one person. You would have to flush toilets all day to use that much in your entire lifetime."

The lady known as Linda was informative and for a little more than an hour explained about the island and buildings before another person took over. This one was a large black man obviously ex-military who let the former president know how things would be in his new life.

"My name is Sergeant Sims. I don't care what you call me because more than likely I won't be seeing your sorry face again in this lifetime!" he barked.

He told the inmate that if he wanted clean clothes he would have to wash them himself. If he wanted to eat any foods aside from the meals delivered regularly which would be pretty basic yet substantial, he would have to cook them himself, grow them or kill the numerous animals or catch fish. There would be no one to watch him and all of that was up to him. He would have a walk in freezer where several animal carcasses would be stored and all of the cooking equipment including an outdoor grill and smoker. Certain areas and rooms at the facility were kept comfortable with a constant temperature including the cell blocks even though he would be supplied with warm blankets. He could go to bed at any time he wished and wake up whenever he felt like it. There might be times when he might want fresh meat of a different sort so there would be plenty of rabbits, rats, birds, sheep and goats to kill with the bow of which he would be given a one hour lesson later on that day. There were also plenty of fish in the cold waters, especially sharks, a fact that was highly emphasized. Videos of people catching and feeding the apex predators, the Great Whites who swarmed the cold waters surrounding the island and were told that these were only eating machines and were essentially his guards. Seals and sea lions he was told were best to avoid as they were often in states of agitation due to their being the primary food of the sharks.

"If you do manage to kill a seal or sea lion, the meat alone from a small one will last you over a month and you might want to learn how to skin one because that would also keep you warm. Don't even think about trying to swim to shore. If the sharks don't get you, the hypothermia will and it's a long fucking swim and by the looks of you, you wouldn't make it far. Actually, Inmate 045, maybe I shouldn't even be telling you this because once you are gone, we can use the island for another purpose but I have my orders to tell you this," said the gruff instructor.

"So I have the run of the place all to myself?" the former president asked.

"Affirmative. There are three hundred and thirty-six cells, no locks and a bed in each. Stay where you like. Personally nobody cares. You can exercise in the recently updated fitness room, run on the track that goes around the island or read. Hell, write your fucking memoirs. More paper and pens than you will ever need or want. Of course, it might only be published when you are nice and dead but that's up to you. It will be the best seller on Alcatraz."

"You are a bastard, aren't you, Sergeant?" the inmate said.

"Hell, why not just call me a nigger? Wouldn't be the first time you've used that word. Compared to you, uh Sir, I am goddamned saint."

Every night there would be a movie projected against one of the outside walls even though even though he was not told they would only be about prisons such as "Escape from Alcatraz, The Great Escape, The Shawshank Redemption, The Green Mile, The Bird Man of Alcatraz, Escape from New York" and others.

After a very basic lunch, he was fitted with boots both winter type and those for the military, sports shoes and ten long sleeved shirts and ten military green short sleeved shirts, five pairs of khaki pants and five pairs of green military fatigues, jackets, coats and then provided with socks and underwear and was told these were to last him one year at which new ones would be delivered with the regular supply shipment. He did ask about suits and was told he had the one he was wearing. When supplies were brought, no one was allowed to speak or even look at him. The personnel were to be gagged and wear dark glasses. The only time a doctor would arrive would be if his vitals started to show some issues and if he did, it will be mostly in silence but for the most part there would be no contact, no human contact. If there was a serious problem, such as something terminal, he would be euthanized and buried in an unmarked grave on the site. A one-hour lesson in archery was conducted with the basics such as how to string a bow and shoot yet it was suggested he practice if he wanted to vary his diet. Three bows of different weights plus one specially designed for fishing along with several hundred arrows and different tips including broad heads were to be included in his life supplies. An additional thirty minutes was devoted to fishing fundamentals and then another to gardening. He was told and shown with videos and pictures that there were only a few places that were easily available for fishing including the main pier where inmates and later tourists came to the island. Of course he could always go online to learn certain skills. Most of the other areas were composed of rocky and steep cliffs. Then he was taken back to his cell, given his evening meal, sedated and was in an even deeper sleep.

Chapter 4

When he awoke the following morning or what he thought was the following morning, he was in a strange place but one that had a familiar look to it. He was on a prison bed on the Island of Alcatraz. Although he had been briefed with information and videos, it was nothing like the real thing so as his eyes adjusted, he began to notice the small details of his surroundings. The odd thing was that it was quiet. Not the sounds of the city by any means with all of the traffic of transportation and people engaged in needless chatter but the sounds of the sea along with the creatures, the birds mostly who had to live there.

As he began to sit up, his shoes had been removed and a light blanket was covering him but he was still in his suit, his very expensive tailored navy blue suit, white shirt and red tie or what they called a "power tie." The pen that he had use to wear that displayed an American flag secured to his left lapel was missing. Aside from that, everything was the same including his watch, its value more than most Americans made in two years was still on his left wrist.

"Well, at least they let me keep the damned watch," he growled along with his stomach begging to be fed.

Continuing to get better adjusted, he noticed a red Thermos on the steel table nearby and next to the toilet with what appeared to be concrete pedestal, a chair of some sort. As he opened the device, the aroma hit him of coffee. It wasn't what he would have normally had in the morning yet was coffee and warm nonetheless which he practically guzzled down. Beside it was a bag with assorted pastries along with an envelope. The numbers 045were scrawled on it the writing in pencil like that of a child.

Loosening his already loosened tie, he began to leisurely munch on the food while reading the contents which were neatly typed on plain paper, no letterhead as it read, "Inmate 045. Welcome to Alcatraz. Your belongings have been placed in the cell to your left. Bows, arrows and fishing equipment are in the cell on the right. Normally with new arrivals to a prison we would mention that if you need anything, just ask but in your case, if you need anything you are shit out of luck. You know what to do and that is live out your life as quickly as you can."

"Bastards!" he shouted.

There was no signature but on a second page was a schedule of when to expect the first delivery of his meals by drone and where it would land and if he was not there when it arrived, it would wait until he did so but since there were other animals like birds and rats, they might get to it first. After the meals were removed, the drone would return to base after a thirty second delay. The days of the other deliveries were also noted for the entire year. In the cell where his personal property including two suitcases, his new shoes were laid out along with a box of vegetable plants and seeds. It was early spring and in the class the day before or perhaps the day before that, he was taught the basics of gardening and shown where the fenced in site was for this purpose. It was an area of about twenty by thirty feet with a gate with a latch to prevent the goats, sheep and rabbits from entering. A small wooden shed was in one corner where assorted tools were stored.

John H. Cary

"We do suggest you do plant and maintain a garden Inmate 045 because after a month or so of eating canned and frozen vegetables, you will begin to crave certain things," had mentioned the instructor.

A nutritionist had told him to take regular vitamins, supplements and medicines which were clearly marked regarding times and dosages plus engage in some form of exercise on a regular basis unless he wished to die a slow and painful death. Even though lazy by nature, he did think it was a good idea especially since he was under the impression that one day he would return to take his lawful place as head of the most powerful nation on the face of the Earth. These thoughts and of how he had been taken to what he felt was a kangaroo court made him angry. His one laptop computer sat still packed away in its case yet there were no plugs. He had been told earlier that another desktop computer was in the library where he could access the internet. This meant nothing so after he had removed his tie and jacket turned on the device to mostly check his emails of which there were none and then he remembered that he would not be able to send or receive any messages so instead he looked through the news which only angered him more as there was no mention of him but plenty of the new leader, the one who in his mind had stolen the election and was obviously responsible for his banishment, his exile and fall from grace. He even checked his accounts of which there were none which angered him even more.

Finally giving up and turning off the device, he changed into the new clothes including the exercise or sports shoes of a famous Japanese company with a distinctive logo along with a jacket and was on his way to explore. At the last moment, he gathered the box containing the vegetable plants and seeds thinking he might as well get them started. There was a small trowel and good knife with a ten-inch blade that resembled one from a movie starring Sylvester Stallone. With no people around, he saw little purpose for such a weapon but decided to bring it along anyway.

"What's going to attack me, rabbits? Seagulls?" he thought and then he remembered that seals often sunned themselves on the rocks on the shoreline to allude the large sharks that cruised the waters of the bay and they were predators so he felt it best to be safe than sorry. "Hell, I've never worn khaki in my life. Look like some fucking peasant. Could be worse. Could be overalls. Oh my God! Army clothes as well? I hate the Army. Good thing I had those bone spurs or somebody did. Kept me from going to Vietnam. Hell, I would have come home in a body bag unless Daddy could have found me some job typing worthless memos. I'm sure the poor bastard that was paid to take my place didn't make it but with money you can buy anything, uh that is except freedom."

It took him a while to get his bearings but in less than an hour he had pretty well figured most of the place out even where the garden was to be. The soil apparently had recently been tilled and was a near chocolate brown in color so he knew it was quite fertile even though his knowledge of horticulture was about as basic as that of a child. He did remember about spacing and soon he had the dozen tomatoes, eggplant and pepper plants in separate rows and then a couple of hills of squash, watermelon and pumpkin planted off to the sides and then a grouping of leaf lettuce and row of green beans which were sown at the base of a convenient trellis. All this was done within an hour and as he stood back, he actually admired his work. Two rows of corn complemented and completed the task. Then, noticing a faucet and length of hose, gave each a thorough drenching before he washed his hands, latched the gate and was gone heading toward another building.

"Farmer Donald," he snickered. "This would be embarrassing if I was a fucking prisoner!"

It had been a long time since he had cooked anything so the meal was very basic. Normally, he would have eaten his steak very well done almost with the consistency of shoe leather but by the time he reached the kitchen, he was nearly starving so entering the freezer, took the Rambo knife from his belt and sliced a huge chunk from one of the cow carcasses and quickly cooked it on the indoor grill to where it was still pink inside. Salt, pepper and a popular steak sauce was generously applied and soon he was at a table eating the heavy protein caveman style mostly with his fingers while licking them and wiping his hands on a towel tucked into his collar.

"Hell, not bad," he mumbled between bites, "not bad at all. I could get to like this. What the hell am I saying? I must be going crazy!"

For several days Inmate 045 spent most of his time exploring his new home. He wasn't uncomfortable and opted not to shave or be too concerned of his appearance. Since he felt that nobody was going to see him why would it matter? When the first drone arrived, he was there and was happy that in some packages there contained fast food and in another a real salad because he had been mostly eating heavy protein in the form of beef and pork. Then when the helicopter landed and delivered the first bi-monthly shipment, he tried to engage the crew in conversation but they went about their business as if he wasn't even there. Still, he was happy to at least see a real person not on a screen. He did notice that he was not allowed to come near the people putting the boxes on the ground which meant he was to put them where they belonged. One machine pistol carrying worker snapped a quick photo and then they were gone but only after a man with a clipboard had gone in the facility apparently to take inventory.

"Well hell! Turning me into a slave. Maybe at least for all of my efforts, I will have something in one of these boxes that tastes like civilization. Wow! There is a God! Two bars of chocolate. Coffee. Nice two, no three whole salmon. I can put them in the smoker or grill at least one of them. Frozen hamburger patties, hotdogs, potatoes…lots of stuff. This will do. Hell, I'll plant the potatoes. If Matt Damon can grow them on Mars old Donald can do it on Alcatraz."

It took time but the inmate did get used to the routine. He didn't necessarily like it and tried to break up the days by attending the garden keeping it in excellent condition free of weeds while harvesting the many vegetables and for days that was all he would eat. He had also started weight training and running along the track that had been installed along the shoreline. By the end of one year he was running for four hours nonstop. His hair was long and white since he had no hair dye and his equally white beard made him look a bit like Santa except he was far from overweight.

There were a few breeches in the security surrounding the island and in the airspace during the first couple of months with several ending in tragedy for those who wished to test the system. Some probably just wanted to get some pictures of the former chief executive while others might have wanted to attempt a rescue but those facts would never be known. As a rather large boat loaded with tourists tried to get a better look inside the zone deemed off limits where buoys were placed at fifty yard intervals, warnings were issued and then shots fired by artillery just missing the bow of the vessel, the first craft made an immediate about face in rapid retreat whereas the second and third continued to move at an even greater speed toward the island despite warnings and single warning shot. These were destroyed as was a helicopter which tried the same tactic.

John H. Cary

This one was serious as soldiers or those in military garb were in the process of repelling from the hovering aircraft just before dusk. The explosive that struck the machine combined with its own fuel lit up the sky like fireworks. Within minutes a clean-up crew came and by the following morning it was as if the breech and destruction had never occurred. After that, nobody tested the system.

One day while he was out hunting, he saw an adult sea lion within range and away from the shore so he decided to try his hand at some big game with the bow. He had read that they were very tasty and that their skins made great coats. He had already killed several rabbits so this was to be an added bonus. After all, what else did he have to do? The shot was perfect and the four hundred pound animal was dead before it hit the ground. Donald Trump, Inmate 045 was becoming a killer.

As he approached the dead mammal, another apparently the mate came charging at him seeking revenge. Later when he reviewed the events of the day in his mind, he still couldn't believe it. The large predator nearly twice the size of the first one came at him even though sluggishly and the arrow he had just removed from the first animal was loaded, drawn and fired directly into the open mouth of the large creature and then the knife came out and made a quick thrust into the back of the animal's head killing it instantly while it fell on the other. He then realized he had his work cut out for him by skinning and preparing the meat.

After more than a month he had learned to fish and was becoming pretty good at it. Having killed several rabbits and was learning how to cure their hides and fur. Inmate 045 was changing. During bad weather he spent his time reading and writing his memoirs but still he was angry especially every time he read the news especially since there was never any mention of himself. The only time he really noticed the passage of time was when the delivery chopper arrived. Actually he was getting tired of the drone deliveries once a week so one time when it arrived, he placed a note in it saying that once a month was okay and that did it. He had plenty of food from the animals he was either catching or killing. Still he was plotting. He had also grown to where he was nearly self-sufficient so when the next delivery arrived he held up his hands in a symbolic gesture of surrender and without a sound handed the armed guard a note stating that once a month would be fine. Then they were gone only to return a month later to the day.

Chapter 5

In a small office located within a large building of an even larger government agency devoted to national security located in the nation's capital, half a dozen computers were arranged with an equal number of workers. It was a nondescript room with no windows yet did have its importance and that was to monitor the activities of certain individuals either suspected of crimes or had been convicted of them and had to be observed. Two, however were strictly devoted to two individuals, the former president of the United States and the second the former first lady who was only observed for her protection whereas with Inmate 045 it was mostly out of routine. Since there was no way he could escape, the job was often boring and the task was typically given to entry level operatives frequently fresh out of college with the hopes of having a stable career as a government employee. At times, there might be an older worker coasting to retirement but that was rare. Turnover, however was not.

"How is he?" asked the supervisor holding his second cup of coffee for the afternoon on a cloudy day just before Christmas.

"Today, the weather has been pretty lousy on The Rock so he has been mostly confined to the gym and library."

It had been nearly two years since the former president had been exiled and his behavior and even appearance had changed dramatically. Donald Trump had gone from a somewhat overweight man in his mid to late seventies with high blood pressure and hair that was constantly being colored to basically a marathon runner of nearly perfect vital signs yet with snow white hair and beard. When he had first arrived, he talked to himself often carrying on conversations for hours on end as if he had an audience but after nearly a year, he had changed mostly in appearance but then another occurred. Apparently someone had left a copy of a book written by a man who had spent two decades in silence, not uttering a word while at the same time earned three university degrees even teaching all while not speaking a single syllable. From that time on, the former egomaniac who was constantly speaking to anyone who would or would not listen had been silent. Before this, if he wasn't making sounds from his mouth, he was either hitting things or stomping around making his presence known. It was if the ghosts of the likes of those former infamous inmates including such notables as Al Capone, Machine Gun Kelly and Robert Stroud otherwise known as "The Birdman of Alcatraz" had returned. His anger was evident. Now, however it was as if he were a ninja of feudal Japan. This behavior confused the workers but it was not their jobs to critique Inmate 045 but only observe and make out their daily reports.

"Here's the report, sir. Nothing of major interest. Up at 4:45. Seems to have found a book on meditation a few months back. He started swimming in the morning about two months ago."

"Swimming? Where?"

"Right, uh there," came the reply pointing to the map.

"For how long? Water's fucking cold from what I hear. He made a suit?"

"No sir. He was in the water naked from these blurry images. It was still dark. Sorry. He was in there for thirty-three minutes. Lucky we have these. Sure wish they had installed a tracking device of some sort but what the hell."

"Must be up to something. Continue."

After showering, spends more than an hour standing not sitting completely still doing his thing before a simple breakfast mostly of heavy protein as you can see. For about ten minutes he wipes down the kitchen, returns to his cell, makes sure it is perfect, not a thing out of place and then he hits the gym for three hours straight before a light lunch consisting of these items, more meditation, then a two hour run and heads to the library before his evening meal consisting of these items. More weights and back to the library and another hour of meditation, another thirty plus minute swim, quick shower and then bed by 10:00."

"Okay, thanks. Does he ever speak?"

"No sir, never. He hasn't said a word in over a year."

"Quite different than when he arrived. Thought we would run out of paper printing out the transcripts."

Inmate 045 knew exactly the day, the date and time so at precisely the stroke of midnight on the last day of the year his second year of exile, Donald John Trump, former United States President plotted and made another major change. He had heard and seen the fireworks in the city on the coast. With a pair of scissors he cut his hair to as close to the scalp as possible along with the beard which had grown halfway down his chest and with his razors, became completely bald with no facial hair. His exercise routine had intensified and gotten to the point to where even though cameras knew of his location most of the time, it was often hard to find him. He had spotted them in the cell block, library, kitchen, fitness center and a few other areas on the island but fortunately a few were obstructed as the vegetation grew. He did take the liberty to add a few for more privacy. When the monthly deliveries arrived, during the first year, he had always been there to greet it but now he was nowhere to be seen.

"Where is he?" the pilot and guard asked.

"He was near you guys a little while ago. Now I can't see him," came the response.

"Where?"

"How the hell should I know? Maybe he turned around and decided to stay away."

"I don't see shit. Fuck this. We're gone! This is too spooky. He was crazy enough when he was president but even crazier now."

As the chopper left, an image emerged from what had appeared to be a large clump of dried grass, a man in standard U.S. Army fatigues, face covered in dirt who began casually gathering the supplies taking them to the kitchen where they were sorted. Little did anyone know but he had begun digging tunnels even though he knew he could not dig his way out of an island. During his first six months of confinement, he had done little to tidy his cell or places where he frequented. The kitchen was often seen a place where piles of dirty dishes sat in sinks and were only cleaned when he needed one to eat from or cook with. It was the same with his cell often going to a different one each night. Trash piled up and insects found scurrying about. Books in the library were left on the tables and papers strewn on the floor. Then for some reason, the place was clean. One evening it was filthy and the next morning perfect. It was not just clean but more like an operating room. Garbage was burned and any material deemed recyclable collected and stored organized according to value and usage. Some of the plastics and metals even melted down and formed into usable bars. The garden was like something from a tourist attraction at a botanical garden. Not only was he a hunter and fisherman having caught one large shark bigger than himself of which he boiled down the jaw, smoked the flesh and made various items of clothing with the skin and weapons from the teeth. Sheep were sheered and fabric made for blankets and sweaters. From what he found online, he learned how to make butter and cheese from the milk of the goats and only once did he use any of these for his dinner and that was when one morning found that one had died during the night. Other than that there became a bond between them as they approached him without fear.

"He's changed. A lot!" mentioned the worker while speaking with his supervisor from the Washington, DC office.

"How so, Sam?" came the response.

"I mean, look at him. Here are pictures when he arrived. Then six months, twelve, eighteen and then take a look at these."

"Definitely doesn't look like a billionaire, does he?"

"No sir, and neither like a former United States president either."

"Hell, I spent ten years in the Army and this guy looks like some of those hard core Special Forces types. Not someone you really want to fuck with. So this is the great Donald Trump, eh? How about printing me those images. I want to show them to the boss before our meeting. How about putting them on disc and have some sort of presentation so you are included since you have actually followed him since he was banished. I'll send you the time. Thanks. Oh, is he still swimming?"

"Yes sir. Twice a day."

"Okay. I will get back with you when the meeting is set up."

The next week, there was a meeting, one strictly devoted to Inmate 045. Entering a conference room the worker only known as Sam set up his laptop and within a few minutes images began to appear on the screen.

"Okay Jack, what do you have?" began Vice Director Michael Payne.

"Director Payne, this is Sam Davis who has been monitoring Inmate 045 since his arrival on The Rock. Probably the one most familiar with this case. Sam."

"Director, I am not going to waste time so let me get to the point. Inmate 045 has changed a lot. You can view these images and determine for yourself. As you can tell, he is nothing like he was two years ago."

"Jesus Fuck! Look at him. The man looks dangerous. Any other thing you have found unusual about him?"

"A few months ago he started swimming."

"Swimming? Where? In that water? It's fucking freezing and there are sharks out there."

"He started for only a few minutes and now is up to more than thirty."

"Why no images?"

"He's either out there at night or early morning so it's hard to take good pictures. Sorry for these being so blurred."

"Is he, uh naked?"

"Yes sir. Totally."

"Maybe he's trying to build up and try to escape but if he gets beyond let's say fifty yards from shore, have someone fish him out. This could be a problem. When he was first put there, nobody expected him to last more than a year at best but it looks like he plans on outlasting all of us. An idea has come up in which we send one of the worst criminals we have and let him loose on the island. He's a condemned man anyway so he is promised his freedom if he kills Inmate 045."

"I'd pay to watch that."

"Well, you will get it for free if once we pull this off. Then we start unleashing the really bad ones with the same promise and well, problem solved. Alcatraz will be a killing preserve."

"That is wicked. Who authorized this?"

"Best you don't know. Public's already forgotten the former President Donald J. Trump anyway so it won't matter. They knew he was a lazy good for nothing bastard, pampered and spoiled with a shitty lifestyle so putting him on The Rock was going to kill him anyway."

"When do we set it up?"

"It's winter. Let's wait until warmer weather. At least we can make it sporty. I'll let you know. This meeting is over. Thanks Jack, Sam. Both of you just advanced in rank and pay."

As the two men were walking back to their offices, they knew or suspected that the former president would soon be dead. They knew that he had started an exercise routine and had altered his diet and attitude but what they didn't know was how lethal he had become. There were places on the island that were missed by the cameras and Inmate 045 had found many of these blind spots as they were called. There, he could train with the knife and bow without being seen. Since he couldn't voice himself in angry messages on social media, he spent time doing research and had begun to learn how to transform his hands and feet into instruments of death as he struck a post wrapped in rope he had found eventually making them as hard as steel. Sam assumed that he would be moved to another department hopefully a bit more exciting although with the new situation, he really wanted to stay at his current position. Jack, however only wanted to see the former leader one thing…dead. He hated the man for many reasons, the main one being that his father had been a contractor for one of Trump's enterprises and had been taken for a lot of money which subsequently bankrupted him. Now he was a broken man, having attempted suicide numerous times and was now in a state mental institution always under heavy sedation.

"I hope he gets it slow and painfully," he mumbled under his breath. "Maybe the convict will rape him for several days and then use pieces of him for shark bait while he is tied to a tree and watches and then when he loses his bait has another piece cut from him. Yeah, he needs to suffer. Bastard!"

Chapter 6

As he stood in his morning meditation, Inmate 045 had a thought. If he couldn't be ruler of a large country, then why not a small one such as Alcatraz? Immediately after breakfast, he headed to the library instead of the fitness area where he began writing his own constitution setting up his own government, his government and country of one.

"I have to set up defenses," he thought.

"I have to prevent any invasion but I also have to allow the supply chopper and drone to arrive because that part of the definition of a state, the third part with it being first a defined area with second with a defined population that third engages in international relations. That chopper and that drone fits this last criteria. Since I am a separate country and they bring supplies, they are technically engaging in international relations. Now, I have got to set up defenses but since I am being watched, I have to do it at night," he continued to think. "Yes, I, Donald John Trump to hereby declare the former Island of Alcatraz to be a free and independent country whereas I am the sole ruler and sole citizen. All visas are hereby denied until further notice. Signed, Donald J. Trump," he thought while he wrote.

Now, the deed was done and he had work to do. Lots of it. From the traps he had set catching rabbits and rats, he had sufficient knowledge of how to catch and kill small animals plus he had become lethal with the bow. Booby traps could easily be made with the materials on the island. It had a lot of trees which meant wood but also plenty of rocks plus more than enough wire and bits of sharp metal. Very simple to cannibalize things in various out of the way places, most of which had no cameras nearby. He had seen enough movies to know that once you kill an enemy, you take his weapons and then kill another and take his and so on. With enough kills, he could build an arsenal. One problem was being able to monitor the entire island. The prison, however was on the highest part of the island so all he had to do was move his quarters to the roof. More than likely if anyone did approach to invade his "country" they would come from the coast but he couldn't afford to assume anything. Moving would be easy but then he began to think that if he moved to the roof, they would think he was up to something so instead, he made a series of alarms mostly with wires or heavy cord on which cans filled with small stones in them that would make noises if touched. He also felt that staying in his cell would further create less suspicion plus would be more comfortable. Setting up defenses would be a challenge considering the size of the coastline. As he was exploring one day, he found a huge cache of building materials including barbed and razor wire that the contractors had failed to remove. With some effort, he placed them in a few areas yet left one with the appearance of being untouched. It was the one near the dock or pier where inmates were delivered and later tourists. Having been a businessman he knew numbers so with his calculations, he felt if he could rig up traps every ten feet or so staggered, he could have it done within a couple of months. Not all areas of the coast, his coast had to be prepared as most of it was too steep and rocky for anyone to access which further helped his calculations. Barbed and razor wire was placed in these. The dock or that place where the prisoners had arrived and later tourists was to be the most heavily defended even though with the appearance thereof. If he placed at least one hundred lethal and the same number of nonlethal traps in that area in a V pattern with the tip of the letter facing the bay, there would be a greater area of carnage. And so it was planned.

Inmate 045 had his work cut out for him. In the meantime, another inmate the notorious serial killer Duncan Tess had just been given a reprieve. Having brutally raped and killed over fifty young boys and girls none over the age of seven he awaited execution or had been awaiting it until two men, men from the government showed up offering him a full pardon along with one million in cash and travel to any country of his choosing.

"So all I have to do is kill one man. One man, that's it?" he began while licking his lips.

"Yes. You will be sent to the island formerly known as Alcatraz where you will kill one man."

"Wait just a fucking minute. The former President of the United fucking States is on that island and you want me to kill that man that pussy and you are going to pardon me and give me a million in cash? Am I hearing you right, shithead?"

"Yes, in two months you will be transported there and when you have done the deed, you will be free. A few stipulations though."

"I'm listening."

"We will provide you with weapons but no guns."

"Knives? I love knives and I can't wait to gut him slowly like a fish. Oh man, to kill the former president of the United States is like a dream. I could put his head in my trophy room."

"Okay, this is what we will do. In two months we will fly you the northern coast of California and take you to within a couple of hundred yards of the island where you will take a small boat and paddle to the shore. A flare gun will be provided so when you end the man, fire it and we will come and get you and then take you wherever you wish to go."

"Good. I can't wait."

"Another thing. You will be placed away from any contact with any inmate as soon as you walk out of this room. You will be given special food and a better place to stay including more comfortable bedding. Hope you like steaks. You will have your own cook and trainer. A week before you leave, you will be given your choice of bladed instruments to become familiar with. Do we have an agreement?"

"Yeah. Fucking A."

With that the most disgusting excuse for a human being was taken from the room while the men talked.

"We really picked a winner with this guy, didn't we?"

"As long as he gets the job done and when he does, we will send in another and another and so on."

"How long do you think it will be until he handles the situation?"

"Couple of hours easily. You know, we could put some of those annoying journalists with either this one or another one and make a deal with the devil to have them killed as a bonus and for more cash. We could give them some bullshit story that they can witness a private hunting preserve and have the exclusive rights while getting a bird's eye view."

"Damn you are good. I think I know exactly the ones you have in mind. We get the criminals to go after each other and then someone just gets in the way of the blade, spear of whatever. Then we stick their bodies in the middle of some protest and, well hell, they died covering a story and became collateral damage."

"Damn I wish I had your mind! You are good!"

"Tell that to wife number four."

Back on Alcatraz, Inmate 045 was planning. He had no idea that he was going to have a visitor yet since he had declared himself ruler of the island, he felt he had to secure his borders. Actually he had no borders except the coastline but that didn't matter. What did matter was the just in case scenario. He had failed in building his wall that he had promised the American people so perhaps now he could prove that he could keep others out. He had come up with a very deceptive way of getting those that were monitoring him to grow used to where he would be for several hours of the night. Since he had started meditating, he changed his location to where he would stand in a certain place or practice the ancient art of Tai Chi in an area near the pier. Then after a week or so, he began working. Already he had started taking various items such as sticks to a place that looked like an area for trash and debris whereas they were components to a series of elaborate traps designed to maim and kill.

Back in Washington, he was noticed but nobody suspected anything out of the ordinary.

"Well Sam, what's he up to today?"

"Meditating at the beach. Same as usual. Don't know why he does it at night and in the morning but he was erratic when he was president and even more so now that he's a convict. Still can't get used to that bald head."

"Well, let me know if he does anything really odd. Not like this isn't. At least in a month, he will be gone."

"Great way to solve a lot of problems…"

The work on Alcatraz continued and soon spring had arrived which meant one thing…Inmate 045 was to have a visitor.

Chapter 7

As warmer weather arrived, several things occurred. First of all, the rather dubious government workers had secured nearly a dozen of the worst of the worst from the penal system. They were costing the tax payers massive amounts of money for upkeep yet polls had begun to show that executions were no longer in favor and if a politician wished to either win an election or remain in office, it was best to oppose such. Most Americans were unaware of the names of these individuals anyway so the only times they were mentioned was when they died or when finally executed. Many times even upon their deaths after decades on Death Row nobody even knew. Having them taken to the island where they would kill another naturally was one of the best kept secrets or was to be the best kept secrets within the government. A dozen were selected out of the twenty-five hundred awaiting execution mainly to have a test to determine the success of this program code name End Mate. Many of these convicted felons were elderly and were on their last legs anyway so they weren't even in the pool of candidates. However, there were others considered "lifers" that had been given as the name implies life sentences often multiple terms due to either the state in which they were convicted had abolished capital punishment or were simply given out said sentence by a more lenient judge and jury. Most of these inmates were even worse than the ones awaiting execution and needed to be removed from the prison population and the planet. Prisoners were always getting in fights and being killed by others so if and when these were to be taken to the island where they would die, their families were told that there had been an altercation and well, these things happen. Also with the pandemic, there was another justifiable method of death and just as believable.

The second thing that was to occur or was occurring had to do with Inmate 045 who had finished his projects with hundreds of booby traps scattered all over the island his island his newly-formed independent nation. Donald Trump had always been a devious and methodical creature of an unpredictable nature which along with his numerous mental disorders made him a very formidable opponent. Now that he had conditioned himself, he was a more worthy opponent even though this fact was well hidden. Those such as Sam who monitored him knew that he had begun an exercise routine yet never dreamed he had become anything remotely related to someone one would consider as deadly.

With the change of seasons there came the day when Duncan Tess was taken to another area even further away from the prison population where he entered a room literally filled with bladed instruments where he was told he could chose as many as he wished within reason.

"How many do you need to kill one man, some old fart like Donald Trump?" he was asked.

After nearly twenty minutes, a total of three were selected including two combat or survival knives, one similar to the one hanging on the belt of Inmate 045 along with a spear of razor sharp tempered steel of the finest quality.

"These will do fine," he said with a sadistic grin.

"We suggest you practice on the targets in the next room and then a week from today you will be taken to the island where you will earn your freedom…"

"And money," the inmate interrupted.

"Yes and money."

"Don't forget my fucking money!"

"We won't."

A green backpack was handed to the man in which stacks of newly-printed one hundred dollar bills were placed all nice and neat which satisfied the convicted rapist and killer.

"Happy?" he was asked.

"Can't wait. Yeah, very happy. Hell, I can go to Thailand and fuck little girls and boys every day and night with all of this."

"Yeah. See you in seven days."

Chapter 8

Duncan Tess was excited. He was excited about not only gaining his freedom but in killing a man he hated. To him this was to be the height of his career. It was to be something akin to having killed the world record apex predator and was certainly one to have bragging rights from. He got to kill the former number one asshole in the world, former President Donald John Trump and was to get paid for doing it. When he had eaten a fine meal of a perfectly prepared steak along with the largest lobster he had ever seen with all of the trimmings, he was given a shot of whiskey that had been laced with a drug of questionable origin and was soon in a deep sleep. When he awoke, he heard the sounds of the sea which was quite different from the pigeons and heavy farm machinery and clank of cell doors in Kansas. Within minutes he knew exactly where he was. His captors or employers weren't concerned about a sneak attack so after a fine breakfast, he prepared with the knives and spear and nothing else because he didn't think he would be gone long.

Soon he and the two men he had met to make the deal still in suits along with one crew member and the ship's captain were heading to into the bay with the ominous beacon, "The Rock" somewhat of an eyesore had a different look and feel to the convict. He felt strange going to another prison but this time not to be locked up but to gain his freedom. As he looked out with his two eyes, somewhat bloodshot due to combination of whiskey from the night before and several cups of strong coffee downed only recently, another set of eyes were looking back at him.

"I see you invader," thought the sole resident of the island. "Come on. A little closer and see what I have for you."

When the boat with a phony sign on the side saying, "Captain Billy's Bay Tours," came within a little more than three hundred yards, the small inflatable lifeboat was pulled alongside for the hunter to climb in. If it had been a normal operation, it would have been conducted under the cover of darkness but no one expected anything more than a simple kill by a man who had extensive experience in the field plus it was someone who actually enjoyed it. Due to the somewhat rough seas, it took more than half an hour for Duncan Tess to reach the pier as he panted for breath from the heavy rowing. He had a canteen of sorts and downed nearly half of it while tying up the boat. The pier was about thirty yards long and had the usual spattering of debris along with the occasional dead gull and silverfish which scattered upon his approach of which he was far from quiet even to the point of announcing his arrival.

"President Trump. Come out come out wherever you are. I am here to play," he sang.

Reaching the end of the concrete pier, he got a reply.

"A visitor. Wonderful! I am waiting up the hill," came the reply.

The minute he reached the end of the structure and began walking up the initially moderate incline just as he put his foot on the grassy hill, he heard a snap and then only searing pain in the muscles just above his knees. He had been impaled by two spikes fashioned from the leg bones of a beef carcass that had been propelled from the trap below the ground. He was in a place out of sight from the awaiting ship and could not be heard even though he began to scream in agony as the heat-sharpened bone had hit bone splintering them nearly lifting the victim off the grass covered soil.

"Mother fuck!" Tess yelled.

"Don't you want to play," came the voice again although this time closer.

"Trump, you bastard!"

"That's President Trump, no King Trump, King Donald the First and I don't believe you have a visa. You cannot come to my country without one so you are an invader. What's your name, invader?"

"Duncan Tess, you fuck!"

"Oh yeah, the child murderer rapist. I heard of you. Normally, I would kill you quickly but you are Duncan Tess. Hum, I think I will just leave you here for a while. No, on second thought I will let you go. Let me take these nasty things out of your legs. If you can make it up the hill I might grant you a visa, patch you up and we can play again."

The sharp bones were pulled out with a great deal of effort and pain making the would be assassin collapse on the now bloodied ground. Inmate 045 then removed one of the knives from the belt of the kneeling convict admiring it along with the discarded spear.

"Nice weapons. Bet you were looking forward in getting me with at least one of them, eh?"

"Yeah but what happened to Donald Trump the billionaire pussy sore loser spoiled brat?" he panted in agony. "What happened to that shitty hair?"

"That was Donald John Trump president of the United States of America not King Donald Trump of the Republic of Alcatraz. Come on follow me up the hill. Maybe you can kill me there with that other knife. Here use your spear as a crutch. There you go. Good. First step, second step, third oh and watch out for the…"

The forth step did it as another group of nine sharpened spikes this time made from the ribs of a cow all affixed to a square piece of wood delivered from several old truck springs impaled the convict but a bit higher just above the belt line entering his abdominal cavity puncturing almost every major organ. It was a lethal blow although death was not to occur for hours as it held the man suspended with his toes just touching the ground.

"Sorry Duncan, I should have warned you about that forth step. Maybe next time they will send a better killer than you. More than likely you will die in a couple of hours because the spikes are actually saving your life. Now if you pull them out, you will bleed to death but if you leave them in we can talk until you die. I haven't talked to anyone in a long time. What would you like to talk about, raping kids, politics, the weather?"

"You fuck!" he tried to yell as blood began to stream from the corners of his mouth along with bubbles.

"Oh hell! You are going to die faster than I had thought. Your lungs are punctured so you will be dead in an hour. Dammit! I was hoping for a long conversation. Tonight I will put you in your boat and let you drift out to sea with the evening tide. Hopefully, your friends in that tour boat will find you. Don't expect to be buried at Arlington. More than likely you will be buried at sea. You were never in the Navy, were you? Oh well, doesn't matter. I know some really big Makos out there who would love to have you as a snack. Okay, go ahead and die while I make out this sign. Paper, paper, oh yes, here we go. Pen, pen, good, found it. Let's see. Sweet and simple."

A note was made out on a rather tattered sheet of paper that read, "Thanks for the company. Next time, please find someone who dies a bit better."

It was signed, "King Donald the First, King of the Republic of Alcatraz."

Just before dusk, Duncan Tess or the body of Duncan Tess was loaded into the craft that he had arrived in. his weapons were removed and the note folded and placed in one of his pockets. With the evening tide, he was set out to sea. Inmate 045 had kept Tess's head as a trophy which he immediately began to boil slowly or on a low heat to remove the flesh. When it was ready, the skull would be placed on a pole at the pier as a welcome for any additional visitors.

Just before dawn, the inflatable boat was spotted and retrieved.

"Tess," came the neutral response from one of the still suited men holding a steaming cup of coffee. "Damn! He died rather badly, son of a bitch. That must have hurt. Trump kept his head. Now that is sick."

"Here's a note, sir," mentioned the other government worker.

"Okay, blah, blah, blah, what? King Donald the First, King of the Republic of Alcatraz? The man's lost it. Okay, activate the next one and while we are at it, let's get rid of those annoying biased reporters. Conservative my ass!"

Meanwhile back on the island, the Republic of Alcatraz, Inmate 045 was having a meeting with his staff which included himself, himself and himself along with a few other selves.

"Gentlemen, sorry to have called you on such short notice but as you are probably aware, we were invaded. Fortunately, the enemy, all one of them was destroyed. Apparently, they sent their best man on an assassination mission. At least we know now that since they sent one, they will send others so we have to be vigilant. What should we do? Good question. Let's ask the Secretary of Defense. The floor is open. More traps? Good idea. Let's make it happen. Huh? Good idea. Add some additional branches to hide ourselves from the cameras. What? Another good idea. Yes, make them subtle and sprinkle some grime to give them blurred images. If we remove them, more will come to fix them. Can't afford to do anything like that. Very smart ideas gentlemen. Let's get on it. Thanks."

The meeting was concluded while another was just beginning in a nondescript building within the center of the capital of the United States.

"Sorry sir, lady about requesting this meeting on such notice," the suited man began.

"Yeah, some request. Kind of hard to refuse when you are escorted from your workplace by men carrying guns and with no eyes and necks. What's this all about or do you intend on telling us before you either arrest or kill us?" asked the famous news reporter.

"You are not in any trouble. In fact we actually need your help and if you can be of assistance and cooperate, this will make you both the most famous people on the planet. What we have to provide is an exclusive story but you have to keep this very hush hush. Actually, we have made sure you cannot and will not tell anyone until after this is over. Okay let's get down to the meat of the situation. Remember former President Donald Trump?"

"Naturally. What about him aside from the fact that he is in exile on Alcatraz?" began the middle aged man with a somewhat squeaky voice.

"Well, we have it on good authority and have witnessed this ourselves that the island is now a hunting preserve. A hardened criminal, remember Duncan Tess?"

"Yes," mentioned the other reporter a lady of also known status.

"Right, the very one."

"Turns out that he was released from prison and promised his freedom plus a ton of cash if he would go there and assassinate the former leader. Unfortunately, he was killed so apparently either the president did it or there are others on the island. We have been told of another attempt to be made within the next couple of days. What we want from you two is to go to the island and report your findings. Under no conditions are you to approach or make your presence known to Mr. Trump now known as Inmate 045. We will place you on the island a few hours before we hear of the other criminal. If you pull this off, you will both be more famous than Jesus. On top of that we will generously pad your accounts and you will also have exclusive rights to other upcoming stories of a more, let's say secretive nature. Do we have a deal?"

Simultaneously, they both shouted their enthusiasm and were told they would be flown immediately to an unknown location and then sent to the island as indicated. Little did they know at in another part of the same building one of the worst serial killers aside from the late Duncan Tess was being fed information but told that he had to end the lives of the two reporters at which he would be paid generously.

"That whiny little bastard I see on the tube all the time?" asked Benjamin Mann, aka Benny the Spike.

"Yeah, this one," he was told along with a photo, "and this one too."

"Oh hell yeah. I'll take her and rape that ass while I bite and snap that tasty neck. I still hate her but you say I'll get five million for all three?"

"That's the deal. Accept or go back to your cell and await execution but the main target is the president or former one."

"Done. I wanted a pardon and he refused probably because I wasn't a paying customer. Mother fucker! Can't believe I am getting paid to do what I would have done for free. Yeah, it a done deal."

"Okay, we will send you back to a more cosy cell and give you menus to order your meals from. Also, you will be shown weapons to select but no guns. In two days you will be sent to Alcatraz where your three targets will be waiting."

The reporters were anxious yet comfortable. It felt strange for them to have no contact with the outside world and had left messages for their fans that they were on special assignments. They had been told to make scripted videos and had explicit orders not to mention anything that would even remotely imply of where they were or what they were doing. Their phones were taken and had no access to the outside world yet were provided with clothing and equipment reminiscent of reporters in war zones which meant military attire, packs, food and even some good knives and other survival gear which made them look like real soldiers to some degree. Then, the night before departure, were briefed and before dawn were taken to the pier silently where they were told to wait and hide in a clump of heavy brush. Each had also been given small but state of the art cameras to film what they expected would gain them every conceivable prize in the field of journalism, photography and journalism. They were instructed where to hide for the best vantage of the approaching battle to come and also to insure their safety. At the same time, Benjamin Mann or Benny the Spike was being briefed as to the exact location of the two. Then just more than an hour after dawn, he began his journey to the pier. Mann was different than Tess mostly because he had served briefly in the Army and understood the lay of the land so when he arrived, he noticed several booby traps almost immediately even tripping one or two just for fun.

"Nice try, Mr. President," he yelled in all directions.

It was easy to spot the reporters but for several minutes did not let on. Instead, he continued shouting and cautiously, methodically moving up the hill. Then he made his move, rushing into the thicket first striking the male reporter with large stone rendering him nearly unconscious. With one down, he grabbed the female pulling her into the open ripping her top showing skin and then he was on her as the sexual assault began. Benjamin Mann was a rapist and murderer like his predecessor but preferred his victims to be dead before he completed the act so as the assault began two items penetrated his victim, one made of flesh and the other of steel. Then, getting up as he had just pulled up his trousers, he began to shout once again challenging Inmate 045. How his intended target ended up behind him is a mystery.

"Looking for me?" came the nearly whispered response.

As Benjamin Mann turned, he felt the cold steel penetrate his belly as it slowly glided its way up neatly slicing his lungs and heart just as a hot knife going through butter. It wasn't the fastest way to die but it wasn't the slowest either. In the thicket, the reporter began to stir, moaning as he tried to get to his feet. As he stood wobbling and bleeding, he was approached by a bald muscular man who he began to recognize as the one who had often said some of the most unkind things of him during his four years in office. There were times, however that he did compliment him but those were few and far between.

"Mr. President?" he said nearly slurring his words.

"No, I am King Donald the First, Ruler the Republic of Alcatraz and I know you and that bitch nice and dead over there," came the cold reply.

"King? Republic? My God, Donald Trump. You killed Benjamin "Benny The Spike" Mann. Let me get my camera."

"Tell you what, why not follow me to my place and you can get all the pictures you want," he said as he began to walk while the reporter fumbled with his gear. "But watch out for the…"

A loud scream was heard about five yards behind the leader at which he added, "booby trap."

Turning around, the reporter stood gasping for breath as the spear from the first convict had impaled him completely through the heart while his arms reached for the weapon before going limp. Three bodies were then placed into the inflatable craft which went out with the afternoon tide. All were missing their heads just as was with the first. Secured to the body of the convict by way of his own knives buried to the hilt in the heart was a one-word note…Next.

Chapter 9

"You know, Trump may not be all that bad," said the agent looking on as the other one stood by while the captain and single crew member laid out the bodies on the deck of the ship.

"How so, sir?" asked his subordinate.

"Look, we know that Inmate 045 killed at least two of these, the male reporter and the con who obviously raped and killed the female. That's a given. We have a good plan here. Let the man do our dirty work for us."

"Do you still want to stick to the story about those two reporters being killed while covering protests?"

"It's a good as any. Who's going to know otherwise? Just flash up some breaking news, have some hero's funeral for both of them and when another gets out of line, we have the same thing with them covering Alcatraz and they get killed racing to a story or they die in the hands of some white supremacist or black supremacist for that matter. The public will buy anything these days. I'm starting to admire Trump. He might be more valuable as an ex-president than Jimmy Carter."

As Sam back in his office in Washington continued to monitor his assignment, he had been updated about the most recent events and was able to gather some very detailed footage.

Alcatraz Awaits: The Legacy of Donald Trump

"How did he know of the construction of booby traps?" he was asked.

"As you can see by some of the reports of late last year, he had found a few books on physics and even though we do block some sites, he found a few others yet oddly enough found out how to make those mostly from movies, even one of the old Conan films."

"Oh, I remember that one. Classic. Now that he's got those set up mostly at the pier, all we have to do is direct the next asshole right into them. You know, just for fun, I might suggest they send two this time or three for that matter. For a man who spent most of his time on the golf course, he sure has turned out to be hard core. I still hate him but am starting to admire the asshole. Keep me posted. Thanks."

"Sir, you may want to take a look at these. Sometimes a drone is sent to see if there are any changes such as construction of boats and such. You know, routine surveillance."

"Wait a minute. Are those what I think they are?"

"You mean skulls on poles? Yes, sir. Looks like Inmate 045 is starting his own trophy case."

"Interesting. Thanks."

"The reports from the other agents with direct contact said the removal of the heads according to the Medical Examiner were like those of a surgeon or a master chef. Each cut was precise meaning there were no re-cuts. They were single cuts without even any slight bone nicks and the report concluded that whoever had done that work was an expert of the highest quality. Hard to believe that someone like Donald Trump, the laziest man ever to hold the highest office was not like he was since he had been banished."

Back on Alcatraz, as Inmate 045 was eating his next meal mostly of heavy protein with several vegetables recently harvested as he sat at the computer reading the news. He had grown used to not seeing his face or anything about him yet now he seemed to be preoccupied with this new hobby, defending his country. He had completed adding to his trophies at the pier and was excited about collecting more. Each skull had a number and he began to fantasize about the prospects of completely surrounding the island, his island with them as a barrier or warning of sorts. With these visitors or invaders coming on a regular basis, he knew he had to intensify his training and keep up his defenses. There were so many items left on the island from careless contractors, his for the picking that he now used to his advantage. Even certain machines were left along with wire, shards of metal and other items he had found most useful. He had continued his training and endurance in the cold waters of the bay and only once encountered a shark but since he was naked, he did not appear like a seal or sea lion plus the fact that he was not splashing or wearing swim fins or one of those black wetsuits. He felt it to be quite stupid to go into the sharks' domain looking and acting like dinner. There were buoys fifty yards from shore that had initially sent him a warning to return or he would be locked within one of the cell blocks but within a couple of months he had found a way to disable the sensors which gave him more freedom which he felt he would need, not to escape but to attack. Inmate 045 had reached the point to where he no longer wished to leave the island but to instead make it his.

When he reflected on his old life, the one of sloth, deceit and debauchery just to name a few, he began to realize these were not qualities of a true leader. Now, he was disciplined of mind and body. He had been challenged during these later years but never in the ones before. In some ways he considered his exile as a blessing and realized that had this not been given to him, he more than likely would have died within a few years

Alcatraz Awaits: The Legacy of Donald Trump

after leaving the highest office in the land. In some ways he knew he was crazy and had practically zero empathy which was making him a very effective killer and defender of his land. There was regret in his life which he had never felt before but perhaps now in his new life, his exile, he could find some source of redemption. He had killed two of the worst convicts in the history of the United States, saving taxpayers millions in their upkeep plus had in at least one way had removed an annoying source of pain within the media possibly two who had amassed a following of mindless minions while pushing and testing one of the basic rights of a free nation, the right or freedom of free speech. He began to hope that more of the same would be sent. Apparently, the United States wanted him dead but couldn't just go right out and kill him so he theorized that in the event he was killed, a story would be fabricated in which one of these vermin had escaped and made it to what they felt was to be freedom, reaching his island where they "just so happened" to come across the former president of the United States and thus ending his life. Then the new government under a man of which he felt was a moron, would sign an executive order, send in a few members of an elite military unit to either capture or kill the intruder but would actually be secretly ordered to do the latter.

"Okay you bastards, you want to play games with me, bring it on. Bring your best or your worst. I will be waiting. Trophies to collect," he shouted under his breath.

Inmate 045 got his wish and more did come. A few days later two were sent who made it halfway up the hill before one was killed by noose made of wire which found his neck nearly decapitating him in the process whereas the other seeing his partner killed in front of him felt the first arrow striking his right shoulder, followed by an identical one to his left followed by one in each leg just above the knee. He then saw an ominous figure approaching clad in camouflage military fatigues walking slowing, knife in hand. It was the Angel of Death. Still, the convict, the paid assassin made one or two futile attempts to save his own life as he began to swing wildly with one of the knives more of a machete at the former president who taunted him for several minutes parrying, dodging while making various nicks to the convict's face and other exposed skin before growing wearing of the game as he dismembered the hand carrying the weapon.

"So, they sent you and your friend to kill me, did they?" he asked.

"I was going to get a million bucks to kill you and then another million to kill the other guy. It was supposed to be easy. You were that golf playing good for nothing selfish lazy asshole, not fucking Rambo!" he gasped.

"No, I am not Rambo. He was a pussy compared to me. I am King Donald and you are…dead!" came the shout as the large blade plunged into the unshaven neck creating a surprised look on the convict's face.

Later on that day, the men in the "tour boat" were monitoring the pier waiting to see some activity were granted their wish although it wasn't what they expected. What they saw was Inmate 045 placing two new skulls on poles. Having done so, he held up five fingers and motioned for them to send that many more.

"He wants five? Hell, we'll send him ten. Got that many waiting to leave right now. Make the call. Tell them that once they kill Trump, the last one standing, gets the share of the others. Promise them ten million dollars."

While the men on the boat waiting for another to bring the ten convicts, they watched at the exiled former leader brought five poles to the pier.

"Confident fucker, isn't he?" mentioned the second in command.

"Yeah, wouldn't it be interesting if he had to go back and get five more poles?"

"Nah, he can't be that good."

Soon two waves arrived and the very second the first group of five had set foot on the landing, five arrows penetrated five necks.

"Jesus fuck!" yelled the leader. "He took out the first five with fucking arrows. Oh shit, look at this…"

The next group were very cautious but were met by their target, one knife in each hand as he waded into them decapitating and disembowelling them all within less than thirty seconds. Heads were removed, bodies placed in the boats and sent back to where they had originated. Before heading back to up the hill he shrugged his shoulders and did something a bit more frightening. Donald Trump fired an arrow making a perfect shot striking the binoculars from the hands of the leader.

"Holy fuck! That was a three hundred yard shot! Tomorrow let's see what he can do with twenty."

This went on for over six months. Sometimes there was only one but often ten or more. During one morning there came an even dozen plus several reporters who all met the same fate. In the late summer, as the inflatable craft was being loaded with three of the ugliest men and one equally vile-looking woman, all armed with assorted knives and swords, just as they had begun to paddle to the awaiting island with greed on their evil faces, a hand came out of the water pulling the one at the bow into the depths followed by the second, then the third and finally the woman, the forth.

"What the hell?" came the response from the captain and crewman looking over the rail.

"They're gone!" they shouted. "Something took them."

After a few long minutes the first headless corpse floated to the surface.

"Look! There!" shouted one of the men in a black suit.

"And there!" shouted the other.

After the third headless body slowly broke the surface, the forth came flying onto the deck.

"Quick! Captain, start the engine. Let's get the fuck out of here. Now!" the one who was considered to be the boss yelled.

"What about the bodies?" stuttered the captain.

"Fuck 'em. Toss this one over the side. Let the sharks have them. If he can get them, he can get us. Go!"

Within seconds, the engines were revved to full throttle while the body of the last convict, the female was dumped without ceremony as a treat to the sharks and other scavengers. Everyone knew that they would never make it to the shore and if any inquiries were made, they would be listed only as "deceased" of natural causes. It was only then when the ship was gone, that Inmate 045 surfaced, a spear in each hand bearing the heads of those he had killed. There was a smile on his face due to the satisfaction that he had added to his trophy case.

During the course of less than a year, more than four hundred had been sent on the same missions with the same promise yet after this last incident, Operation End Mate was cancelled. Naturally this was not known to the one who had been the reason for it so he continued to train and prepare. The former president of the United States was no longer a walking heart attack or stroke but was instead the picture of perfect health. He was, after all, King Donald, King of the Republic of Alcatraz. After a busy morning, having returned to the island, fed himself a large nearly raw steak, taken a shower and changed into dry clothes, he began to feel tired, sleepy so a nap was justified. Soon he was in a deep sleep.

Part 2

Chapter I

"Donald? Honey? Are you going to sleep all day?" came a voice, a familiar one, one he knew quite well.

"Honey?" the voice repeated as it shook his shoulder lightly.

"Huh? Where am I? Are you my, uh, really my uh, uh wife?" he stammered.

"But of course. Who else would I be? You don't know where you are? That must have been some dream you were having. It's okay. You are home, here in north Florida."

"Florida? Not Alcatraz?"

"Alcatraz? No of course not. What gave you that idea?"

"It was just dream. Come here. Come closer so I can look at you. Oh my God! You are so beautiful! If I'm having a dream now, I hope it never ends."

"You haven't said anything like that to me in years."

"Well, those words are well overdue. Come to me, my darling."

"Don't you want breakfast?"

"No, I want you."

Soon the former president and first lady were in the heat of passion with more to come later in the day. It had been just a dream, a vivid dream, a life changing dream. He had not been banished. He was not a killer but the dream left an impact on him.

As he entered the kitchen the smells were almost repulsive. It was the scent of everything unhealthy. Fried foods of every sort. Eggs, bacon, sausage all overcooked. As he looked down at his plate which had now been set at the table, he nearly gagged.

"What's wrong, sir?" asked the cook a puzzled look on her face.

"I'm sorry. Nothing wrong but would you mind if I had something uh, less fried. Do we have any fruit or something like that? I mean, something with less salt and fat. For some reason, this no longer appeals to me. I would appreciate it. Very kind of you and I appreciate your effort. Thanks."

"Healthy? Less salt and fat? Thanks? He never thanks anyone," thought the cook with a reply of obedience.

"Excuse me uh, uh…"

"Martha."

"Yes, Martha. Do we have an agent named Sims?"

"Yes, Mr. President. He is on duty now."

"Would you mind asking him to come and see me in an hour?"

"He forgot my name. What's wrong with this man?" the cook thought again.

"Certainly Mr. President. I will fetch him."

"Martha, I hate to be a bother but would you mind not calling me that name anymore?"

"What name, Mr. President?"

"That one."

"You mean Mr. President?"

"Right. That one."

"Very well sir. What name do you prefer?"

"My name is Donald. Please call me that one or Donny but no more Mr. President. I wasn't very good at that job so I don't think I am deserving of the title."

"Very well, Mister, I mean Don, Don, Donny?" she gasped.

"Thanks. Whenever Agent Sims is available will be fine but in an hour I will be ready. I think I will just take a quick shower and then walk around for a bit."

"Very well Mister, I mean Donny."

As Donald Trump was leaving the kitchen, the first lady was entering but not before she was literally grabbed as a passionate kiss was planted on her lips. After catching her breath, she let into the cook.

"Martha, did you just call my husband Donny?" she growled.

"Yes, Ms. Trump."

"How dare you disrespect him? I've a good mind to fire you!"

"Honey! I ordered her to call me that and wouldn't mind for every other staff member to do the same. I was a shitty president and see no need to be referred to as someone who actually deserves the title. Obama? Now he was a good president and the one that beat me in the election. Now he is a good man. In fact, I am going to call him just as soon as I finish my shower. Martha, please take the day off. I'll cook. Here, here's a couple of hundred. Do something good for yourself. See you when you get back. Have fun."

"Oh thank you Mister…"

"No, no, no. It's Donny, remember? Go!"

"Honey, do I have anything on my schedule today. What day is it, anyway?"

"You don't remember the day? Are you alright? Let me call the doctor. It's Saturday so you really don't have anything planned unless you wanted a round of golf. What did you have in mind? Are you sure you are alright?"

"Never better. Let me take a shower. Care to join me?" he winked.

A shower and another round of passion even though a quick one but one nonetheless and he was ready for his day. Everyone found it odd that instead of his usual suit or what was called upper casual meaning no tie, he came out wearing jeans and a t shirt.

"I do need a haircut," he mentioned to his secretary who on Saturdays only worked half a day.

"Very well. I will have him come this afternoon."

"Thanks uh, uh,"

"Cindy."

"Yes, thanks Cindy. Also would you mind placing a call to the president?"

"Please give me a few minutes, Mr. President. Sir, I was told by Mrs. Trump that you wished to be called Don or Donny. I have to hear it from your own lips and will make a formal notice to all employees."

"Yes, Cindy. My name is Don or Donny."

"If you will wait in your office I will patch the call through."

"Thank you Cindy. I will be waiting."

A few minutes later the call did come through.

"Mr. President, Donald Trump here."

"Good hearing from you, Mr. President," came the reply from the Oval Office.

"First of all, my name is Don or Donny. I was a lousy president so I would prefer to avoid the other title."

"Lousy or not, you still deserve my respect."

"As you wish. First of all I want to apologize for my behavior toward you. I lost the election fair and swear. You won. Congratulations. Secondly, I am calling off the dogs that are still loyal to me. You've got great ideas and I hope that everyone will support you. Third? Well, there is no third. I am deeply sorry for the trouble I have caused. Congratulations once again to you and your second in command."

There was some brief small talk and questions if the former president was feeling well and then the call ended. Another couple of calls were made to some of his bitter enemies in the United States House of Representatives and other places and he even added that he would have to prove his sincerity and had no intension of calling a press conference and even cancelled all of the rallies he had planned with no explanation. Then it was time to speak with the Secret Service agent known as Sims. Donny, as he was now being called was strolling around the grounds of his home, having spoken with the grounds keeper who lived on site about tilling up an area that could be used as a vegetable garden in one spot and flower garden in another. He also asked the kindly Asian worker to contact a company to install a greenhouse for the wife and flower garden. Then it was the agent's turn who approached him trying not to appear confused.

"Mr. President, Agent Sims reporting as ordered sir," came the formal and obedient introduction from the large black man with an intimidating shape and demeanour.

"Relax Agent Sims and from now on you will address me as either Don or Donny but none of this Mr. President bullshit. Am I clear? And that is an order."

"Very well Don, sir. How may I assist you?" he asked coldly.

"You don't like this job, do you?"

"I am an agent assigned to protect you and will give my life in my duties."

"But you don't like me, do you?"

"I am an agent assigned to protect you…" he repeated before being interrupted.

"Sorry to interrupt but you were in the Army, weren't you?"

"Yes Mister I mean Don, sir. Ten years."

"Wonderful. Sergeant wasn't it?"

"Yes uh Don."

"Excellent! I need your help."

"Anything. How may I assist you, sir?"

"I want you to train me."

"Sir?"

"Sergeant Sims, I want you to train me like a new recruit. I want you to treat me like shit. I want you to work my ass off. I'm going to temporarily reassign you strictly for this purpose. First of all, you and I are going shopping. We are going to buy me a new wardrobe just like the one you had for ten years. I know I was very disrespectful to members of the service and even avoided the draft but I feel a need to make up for all that crap. Will you help me?"

"If this is what you want, I will obey."

"Obey nothing. I want you to hound me you and you alone. From now on, I am in the Army. I am your bitch. I need fatigues, boots, the works. My hairdresser is coming this afternoon and this mop I call hair is history. Shaved just like yours. We have a fitness room but I want it upgraded and I want you to be in charge of that. You are to tell what you want or what I need because I want to go hard fucking core. Your job is to make sure I never quit. If I drop dead, make sure I do it in push up position. If you let up on me one tiny, tiny bit I will be on you like stink on shit. You are to talk with the cook to make sure I eat what you eat."

"You're serious, aren't you sir?"

"As a heart attack. I will have my secretary make up the orders. Let's get the shopping done and also keep this out of the press. I don't want this to leave this compound. Are we clear?"

"Crystal."

"This is not some fucking publicity stunt. Not a word of it leaks out."

By the end of the day, a large supply of fitness equipment had been ordered and set up. Along with the equipment, Donald Trump was outfitted with a completely different wardrobe including jeans and casual attire plus military clothing. One thing that was of greater importance was the hairstyle. When the hair dresser arrived he was when he asked, "Mr. President, just a trim, sir?"

The reply of "shave it" came as a surprise.

"Sir?" he asked, "did you say shave it?"

"Yes. Get rid of it all. I want it just like the sergeant's," he pointed.

"Very well but you can't hold me responsible if you don't like it."

"If you don't wish to do it, either I will or my large friend over there will. Up to you."

The hair dresser did as he was told. When Mrs. Trump entered the room just as the last stubble was removed she literally screamed.

"Donald? Why?" she asked after calming down.

"Time for a change. I was focusing on this hair and also on golf. No more to both. Oh and Tim," as he addressed the stylist while giving him a huge tip, "I want the sergeant over there to check your phone and if there are any pictures in it of me and my new style, they will be deleted. You will also not mention this to anyone. Are we clear?"

"Very clear, sir."

The sergeant did as he was told. It was approaching mid-afternoon when everything had been set in motion.

"When do you want to begin, Don?" asked the sergeant now growing used to the new name of his boss.

"Yesterday. Let me change. The doctor is coming over to take some blood and other liquids but fuck what he has to say. If my wife wishes to join in, so much the better. If not also so much the better. Nobody will ever call me a wimp or pussy after you finish with me. I'm in boot camp, right?"

"Right Don. For the next eight weeks you will suffer. I will wake up at 4:30 every morning. You will be told when to eat, sleep, shit, everything. Welcome to hell. As soon as the doctor finishes with you, it will be my turn. You may regret this but if you survive, you will be a lean, mean fighting machine."

The doctor did come by, did a quick check and gave his approval for an exercise routine but had no idea what kind of routine his patient was to endure. Then it was the sergeant's time.

It seemed as if the very second the last lace was tied on the boot, the yelling began. The sergeant had changed into his own uniform or what he wore as a drill instructor only a couple of years ago. Everyone on the property had been informed as to what was going to take place but some including who was to be called Don regarding his wife, had no idea as to the extent of the harassment and exercises. The dream had been more than just vivid but was as if he had actually lived that life. Never once did Don complain and followed orders to the letter. Since the exercises which began with an hour of being yelled at and called every name in the book with the idea that you had to break down the recruit to build them up. It surprised the sergeant that at no one time, did the former president back down or even flinch. He stood at attention, eyes straight ahead as the one in charge violated his personal space. Then he was ordered to the treadmill which was the best one ever made. Not only did it alter its angle as if the runner was going up a hill but also changed speeds. There was a screen in front in which objects appeared to be thrown at the runner making him dodge and slightly trip but never did Don let up and for two hours while carrying a pack that began with twenty pounds continued to push himself much to the surprise of the sergeant.

After the run, came the weights for an hour before the exercise was over. Then it was dinner consisting of high protein with steaks that were considered medium rare instead of well done. The only seasonings were salt and pepper even on the baked potato and garden salad which were all eaten within ten minutes. After that it was time for a shower and instructions on how to shine the boots, press the fatigues and then bed. The bedroom was one place where the sergeant opted not to go except for the early morning wakeup call. Despite the intense four hours of heavy training, he had time and energy to love his wife as it seemed they were rekindling their marriage.

 The next morning just before 4:30 all hell broke loose as the sergeant burst into the room shouting at the top of his lungs at the sleeping "recruit." He hardly noticed the wife as she leaped out of bed completely naked although did give her a thumbs up as he was leaving with her husband in tow struggling to get dressed.

 "Up and face the world maggot!" Sims yelled.

 "What no comment?" he continued.

 That was one thing that surprised the agent in that never once did the recruit say a word unless requested to do so. For the next four weeks day in and day out, the training continued. Donald Trump had lost a lot of weight and was actually not only gaining muscle but displaying what one would consider a six pack. He had a flat stomach while also maintaining a somewhat calm demeanour. After that intense month of training, he did make a request to the sergeant of wanting to learn how to use a bow and a knife. The best archer in the world was in Denmark, however the second best was in nearby Alabama and initially declined the job yet when told how much he would be paid, realized it would have been stupid to turn something like that down. Businesses including his had been in trouble due to the pandemic but with this kind of money it was salvaged and then some.

John H. Cary

There were so many parts of the dream that he wished to fulfil. In the other life, the dream, he had been responsible for his own training but in this one, he had others to help him. It was strange that before the dream, he was basically a worthless man living a worthless life and he didn't even know how worthless it was but now he felt he had a chance of redemption. The law suits that had him occupied ended without him having to serve time in prison but instead had wiped out his businesses and to settle them including back taxes, had to sell most of his real estate. Fortunately, some of his children were able to purchase several parcels of property, allowing him to live on one of them. They had considered the southern part of the Sunshine State but land was cheaper and there were more secluded areas for a former president to live out his life similar to that of the thirty-ninth president in the northern section. It was large and secluded with high walls and fences so security was an easy matter plus the fact that there weren't any neighbors anywhere near the area. The house wasn't as large as ones he had occupied before but it was comfortable and he appreciated the simplicity. When he was not running for hours on end on the treadmill, he was running along the perimeter of the property and in both cases carrying heavy packs eventually up to nearly one hundred pounds. Also, the romance between him and his wife was developing like it has never been before and they were actually beginning to fall in love with each other again. Sometimes the media tried to find out what was going on with the former president mostly because now he was silent. There were no late night or early morning angry messages on social media and at times they tried to irritate him by making up stories they knew were not true just to get a rise out of him but were now unsuccessful.

After a few weeks of training he was up long before the sergeant was and sometimes was standing at his bed waiting.

"Up and at 'em Sergeant Sims. We are wasting daylight," he said one morning.

"Daylight? What time is it?"

"3:30. Time for training."

"Okay, get to the treadmill program eighteen. I will be right there. Jeez!"

Eight weeks of intensive training which simulated basic training or boot camp as it was called came to an end yet Don insisted it continue. The archery instructor came at that time and was a guest for several weeks. He brought along several different types of bows yet assumed that his pupil who even though had never met was impossible not to know to some degree. The instructor had even voted for him twice and felt it to be an honor to be spending time with such a celebrity. He expected an old man, rather pudgy in the middle with an odd color to his hair but what he found was a completely bald man in top condition with a preference for military attire.

"We can have a plane come and pick you up if you like," mentioned Don during a conversation on the phone.

"No, Mr. President, I will drive down there if you like. I was planning a vacation on the coast anyway and have a couple of relatives that I haven't seen in a while."

"Suit yourself. You know I am unfamiliar with archery at all so please bring me several models with various pulls and we can decide which is best for me but make sure you bring some heavy ones as well since I have been exercising lately."

"Will do, sir."

Naturally, when they met, he realized by the size of the former president's arms, he might be able to handle some of the stronger bows he had brought along and was glad he had the forethought to have done so. As he got out of the vehicle after it and the gear and luggage were thoroughly searched by the agents, he asked where President Trump was.

"Here," came the reply from a man who sounded like the former president yet did not have the appearance.

Introductions were made and it was agreed that the first lessons would begin the following morning. A tour of the property was given along with the garden in which a bucket of fresh vegetables were harvested. After the instructor was settled into his quarters, he heard the sounds of training. It was as if he was on an Army base. When he followed the sounds to the source of the shouting, he saw a large bald black man shouting at the former president. Already he had been surprised at the change in appearance of his client and that he was to be called Don or Donny but seeing him being yelled at while he pressed enormous amounts of weights completely floored him.

"Don you shit. Don you fucking pussy. Hell, my mother can lift that. It's only four hundred pounds you pussy! Come on eight, nine. Don't you quit you mother fucker! One more. Almost. Good. Just about there. Perfect. Now let's go for four fifty."

This and other exercises continued including self-defense, knife training and pounding various items from a rope-covered post to a cinder block wall. What he witnessed was nothing like what he expected or had seen during the four years of a failed presidency. The transformation was something out of novels yet as he watched the man train, he began to admire him.

As the instructor named Byron gathered in the kitchen later that afternoon or early evening, another thing that surprised him was seeing the former president cooking.

"I didn't know you were a cook, sir," he mentioned as he sipped a fine imported beer while the sergeant did the same and the wife looked on.

"Just started. Felt I needed to get my hands dirty. Hope you don't mind something simple. Steak, lobster, baked potato, salad alright?"

"Oh perfect!"

"Maybe it would be best if you cooked your own steak because I'm not sure how you want it. You can have any cut of beef you want. I'm having a couple of sirloins but we have some whole beef carcasses in the freezer. Just let us know. Oh, we have some nice shrimp and scallops that were caught this morning. Thought I might skewer some up and put them on the grill. If you want something else, that will be fine."

"Oh no, this is wonderful! You eat two steaks, sir, uh Donny?"

"I do when I am bulking up. Same with the sergeant here. He works for the Secret Service and I kind of pulled him off regular duty for a while. Just felt I needed to get in better shape. I know you were surprised with the hair, right?"

"That was one item, yes. Do you mind my asking why? I mean, why did you decide to go that route?"

"There was just too much damned focus on it. It was real hair but not real color and with the better body, I don't think it would suit me."

The conversations were casual in the kitchen and at the dinner table. In some ways, Donald Trump seemed like a very rich man or formerly one but in others he was a bit crude, sometimes eating his steak with his hands and licking his fingers while at other times, knowing the exact utensil to use on the lobster and other items.

"I used to eat any cut of meat very well done almost like shoe leather," he mentioned.

"That's what surprised me but those steaks are just barely medium rare and you seem to only season them with salt and pepper," mentioned Byron.

"Good eyes. No point in spoiling good meat. Now, a bit of warning ahead of time. We tend to begin the day early. Usually around 4:30 we are up and training but would like to take the full afternoon with you to begin my lessons. There's a range set up the furthest target at one hundred and fifty yards. Sure would be nice to have that guy from Denmark here with you and wish that Howard Hill was still alive."

"You contacted the Dane?" asked the Alabama native.

"Too busy plus still some hotspots with the bug. Just glad you could come."

Conversations continued until right at 9:00 when Don had to go to bed yet his guest was told he had the run of the house and if he needed anything, he could contact any staff member including the guards or just make him whatever he wanted in the kitchen or he could fix it himself. Sleep came after some heavy passion between the couple and soon the following day arrived.

For two solid weeks, every afternoon just after lunch, the training began. What surprised the instructor was how quickly the student learned.

"Don, so you have never used one of these?" Byron asked.

"I think I had one of those with the rubber tips when I was a kid. It came with an Indian headdress so you could play cowboys and Indians. From what I remember, I shot one of my aunt's vases and knocked it off the shelf breaking it to pieces. It was probably worth a fortune but she never said a word. Knowing me, I probably blamed it on my brother and he more than likely took the blame. I was probably as bad a child as I was an adult. Just never felt the need to use one of the real things plus you can't cheat in archery like you can in golf," he snickered yet at the same time was embarrassed.

"Sir, I have been watching you for the four years you were president and then the reality show but during all that time,

I don't think I have ever heard you admit you did anything wrong. It kind of confuses me. Maybe in public when everyone is watching, you are one person but in private, you are different."

"No Byron, I think I was an asshole in both situations. Maybe that's why I've been married so many times. Now that I've had time to reflect, I am surprised that I was every elected in the first place and also that anyone would have married me for anything besides my money. I guess I just conned my way into the presidency. Been doing that all my life."

"I guess this and your change in appearance will be a good publicity stunt for you if you don't mind me saying so."

"Nobody knows. In fact, I haven't even watched the news in ages and as you can see, I don't have my phone and haven't commented on social media since God knows when. As you know in your contract, you cannot share any pictures or information with anyone. You will get some nice mementos of our time together plus a shitload of cash and I will even give you a new car of any type you like within reason of course meaning no Lamborghinis but no, this is not for anything but for me. Okay, I'm being selfish. I want to learn something and have found that personally I hate and always have hated golf. Boring as hell but rich people do it. Why I have no idea. Grand waste of time and real estate when you come to think of it."

"Sure didn't expect comments like that," the instructor thought.

"With this, it requires patience and skill. One thing I want to learn is how to hit moving targets like you and the other guy can do but like the sergeant, I want you to push me and push me hard regardless of how long it takes. If you can stay more than two weeks, fine because I will make it worth your while but I will understand if you have other places to go."

"Understood, sir."

John H. Cary

The hard training with the archery instructor continued for a full month and it did amaze him as to fast he learned even to the point of developing skills beyond his own. When he realized he could no longer teach Don anything new, he departed. A new foreign luxury SUV was provided along with a briefcase filled with cash plus full insurance coverage for several years and maintenance.

Chapter 2

Donald Trump had changed more than anybody anyone had ever known but the odd thing was that only a few people actually knew. Even though he had asked former Agent Sims to train him for at least eight weeks, he requested that he continued to do so on a permanent basis with a guaranteed salary of half a million per year with half that much paid up front in cash as a bonus of which the sergeant felt it stupid to turn down. He was still listed as a Secret Service agent on special assignment which meant retirement benefits at a later time.

It was odd that the two had become friends, real friends yet Don continued to make sure he was treated as a client grunt and despite his current or former celebrity status, made sure that the sergeant never let up on him during training.

Agent or Sergeant Robert Sims was a black man. He was not just black as in having a chocolate brown complexion but was actually black reminiscent of the nameless drill sergeant in the Tom Hanks' movie "Forrest Gump." Robert, even though hard core due to his Army life and the fact that he had come from humble beginnings, was a good man. He had been married but it was short-lived and he blamed himself and saw no point in passing it to his ex-wife. Fortunately, he had produced no children so when the marriage ended and it came time to re-enlist, he opted out and within a few months was recruited by the United States Secret Service initially guarding senators and congress personnel yet due to his diligence, he was soon transferred to his current assignment. Initially, he and the other agents in charge considered it to be a punishment detail but all were assured that it was to be only temporary plus they were given extra pay and more vacation time along with other perks. At first, he hated his client because he considered him a liar, cheat, racist and host of other negative adjectives. When he was ordered to begin training him, he felt this was a perfect opportunity to do what everyone else wanted to and that was put him through hell. This, however changed when he soon discovered that this vile individual was not what he had expected and was sincere especially after the first two weeks and when he was told not to let up for one moment. It seemed like the more he pushed, the more he wanted to be pushed often getting to the point of being pushed back. After nearly six months, he realized he was creating a monster, someone he was having a hard time keeping up with so they ended up training each other. This was no longer the lazy, wasted life, selfish asshole with a following of brainless minions but a completely different individual.

"Don, I have to apologize to you," he began one day as they were having lunch in the greenhouse while his wife worked on some orchids on the other side of the structure.

"How so Sergeant?" came the reply.

"First of all, my name is Robert. Secondly, I had initially thought of this as some bullshit Donald Trump publicity stunt but you have made it clear that this was not to be mentioned on any social media outlet and you have had no rallies since all this began. I mean, look at you. Goddamned! For a man in his seventies, you are in incredible shape not just for your age but for any age. I never thought I would ever say this about you but I have to admit that I admire you and actually consider you as my friend."

"Robert, you know that's probably the nicest thing anyone has ever said to be other than my wife saying for me to fuck her again," he whispered especially the last part.

At that, they both began to laugh nearly to tears while also embracing. The training continued hard and heavy for another month. Often Robert would attack Don when he least expected it and at all hours of the day and night.

"Don, you fuck! I just killed you and your whole fucking family. You are toast you shit! Don't you dare let up for one second? Death is serious. This isn't golf where you can try again with some penalty. This is life and you have only one shot. I swear to Christ, that the next time will be a whole hell of a lot more and soon I will be using more than some piece of wood against your sorry ass. What if I decided to do this on your wife or kid? Bet that would make you realize this was no fucking game. We have got to get your senses in better shape. I know just the man who can do it. Little Okinawan bastard. Let's give him a call and get him over here. Humble as hell but I bet if you offered to send a crew to his village to do some major upgrades on sewers, roads and such plus install a shitload of solar and wind power things plus help out the schools, he will jump at the chance. Oh and also pay him a wad of cash. Are you okay with this?"

"I can start sending the crews in there yesterday."

"Now don't let this guy fool you, Don. This fellow's a cross between a super ninja and a Shaolin priest. In fact, he probably is one or both. You think I have been putting you through hell. Consider that a picnic. For let's say four months, he will challenge you more than you can only imagine. His name is Ho as in ho-ho-ho but this is no Santa Claus. Let me get on the horn and start moving. Now, we don't have to do this, you know. Just tell me and I will forget it."

"No, Robert. Make the call. I feel I need this. I also think I need to be trained with a gun. What is your opinion on that one?"

"Okay, I agree with you on that one but first let's get Ho over here. The gun will be the easy part but by the time he finishes with you, you might not need one."

While they were waiting on Ho to arrive, more conversations were held including one in which Don inquired about Robert's education.

"Robert, just out of curiosity, what kind of education do you have if you don't mind me asking?"

"Well, before my entry into the service, I earned a master's in history specializing in the United States Constitution. Then after I had advanced in rank to sergeant I was fortunate to be stationed in Massachusetts where I ended up with a law degree of all things from Harvard."

"Jesus Christ!"

"Don, you will find that most of the agents have this kind of degree. I speak three Asian languages and can get by in Hindi."

"Hell, I cheated my way through school. Lazy and worthless but when you have money you can buy anything. To this day I am still amazed that I didn't end up being a dog catcher but probably would have failed at that. Seventy something years of being an idiot. The only one who has ever been honest with me was you."

Chapter 3

How Ho even found the residence is one thing but how he entered it without being detected is another. The thing is though that when the cook, Martha arrived in the morning, there he was sitting at the table nursing a cup of coffee.

Noticeably startled, she immediately offered the small or actually petite Asian man breakfast which according to custom was declined yet when offered again, accepted. Preparing a meal was now a treat especially since Don had opted to cook his own yet told her that he did want her to continue with him even though her duties had lessened to a large degree so when she was not preparing her boss's meals, she was helping out the agents'. The lady was kind and well-liked and it just seemed that she was part of the fixtures so even though there was a lot less for her to do as far as filling what was listed in her job description, she did perform other duties such as working with the former first lady in the greenhouse and harvesting vegetables from the garden. She was told that she was welcomed to take as much home to her family as she wanted.

After about ten minutes, Ho had completed his meal and was told that it would be easy to find the former president who she naturally assumed was who he was there to meet. Perhaps he was assigned to teach him Japanese or martial arts although he didn't look dangerous.

"The president who has ordered the staff to call him Don or Donny is more than likely in the fitness center she said, while washing the plate and bowl in the sink. As I said, he is easy to find. Just follow the shouting," she said casually.

When she turned, he was gone like a puff of smoke. Within minutes he was standing behind the sergeant as a string of profanities continued to flow as he spotted the one on the bench while the bar began to bend with the weight of over five hundred pounds.

"Come on you weakling! My grandmother can do better than that. Is that all you got? Come on. Nineteen. One more. Push it. Feel the burn. There you go. Got it! Now, let's see if you can do five hundred fifty," he said walking over to get another plate from the stand. Only then did he see his friend.

"Mr. Ho. My God. Some people never age," came the warm greeting. "Here, let me introduce you to the former president of the United States, Donald Trump."

"Mr. President."

"Don or Donny, please," came the reply.

"Very well Donny. I am Ho. You can call me uh Ho," the Asian responded in a thick Japanese accent. "What happened to your hair and the fat?"

"Gone along with hopefully the ego and attitude. Welcome. Sorry but I wasn't told of your arrival. Did one of the agents pick you up at the airport? I must have missed the memo."

"No, I arrived early this morning. Kind of startled your cook, uh Martha I think was her name. I think your security needs a bit of an upgrade. I just let myself in."

"Wow! You are good."

"Told you," mentioned the sergeant adding another plate.

For a better part of an hour, talk was casual yet productive as the new instructor mostly watched to find weaknesses in his new client who was strong by any standard yet weak in others. Finally he said, "I can train you. It will not be easy but I can assure you that by the end of six months, you will be so lethal that your skills will frighten yourself but you have to do exactly as I say, no questions asked. Agreed?" he asked extending his hand.

"Agreed," came the humble reply.

Instead of hitting the treadmill for a hard two hour run with a full pack, he was told to remove his shoes, close his eyes and stand in the corner, back to the wall and listen. This went on for well over an hour. At a few times, he was asked what he heard. At first it was the activity going on outside but then he began to hear his own breath and the beat of his own heart and even to some degree that of the sergeant and Ho, himself.

"Never known one to pick up that during the first try. Looks like we have one we can really train," Ho mentioned to his friend.

The next couple of months were nothing like Donald Trump had ever experienced in his life. The physical training was tough but this was different. It involved stilling the mind and becoming more focused. At first he was told to stand and clear his mind and remain in that position for as long as he could. Initially, it was for one hour but then as he expanded his mind, he began to see images, people, lights and other things. Time meant nothing to him and eventually when he opened his eyes, he realized that he had been in that state for a full day and then for two days. When he got to where he could stand without the feelings of the passage of time nor of his body, Ho took him to a different level. Since he had gotten to where he could shut down his physical senses, that meant he could ignore pain and with this ability he could focus on his immediate surroundings which became smaller and smaller. Eventually he found he was able to harness energy and even to where he could move objects.

"How can he do that or does he even know what he is doing?" asked the sergeant.

"When you told me who you wanted me to train, I thought I was going to be working with an idiot and a lazy one at that but this one is different. We are filming this aren't we?"

"Everything in this house is being monitored except for the bedroom. Can't wait to review these?"

"There is more to this Don fellow than what we had expected. Robert, you must have done a great job conditioning the body so it looks like we opened the doors to the mind. Now that he can do that unconsciously, it is time to get it to where he can do it consciously. I'm sensing we need to get him a pet. I also feel we need to get one for the first lady but different. Yes, different from any pet you can imagine. I am sensing a place nearby, no two places nearby. One saves animals that have been abandoned by their mothers and the other has an animal that starts with two of the same letters. Sorry but I don't know your words. Is there an animal one with a kind of long neck with two l's beginning its name and the other is a cat but not an ordinary one. This begins with a p."

"Ho, the only ones I can think of are llama and puma."

"Yes, those are the animals for this couple."

At dinner that night after a hard day of heavy training mentally and physically, Don and his wife looked at the tapes showing how the former president was standing and then like a character in the films by George Lucas began to float off the ground and also move the sports equipment even the heaviest weights off the floor.

"I did that?" he asked in a very surprised manner.

"Film doesn't lie," mentioned both Robert and Ho.

"Honey, do you remember when you woke up one morning and acted as if you had no idea where you were?" asked wife holding her husband's hand.

"Yes, of course. I didn't know any of the staff." At that point he began to explain of what he had dreamed. There was the trial, the divorce, the exile and then the training, meditation, learning archery and then the numerous kills from those convicts sent by the government. "Hell, Robert you were there."

"On Alcatraz?"

"No but you were one of the people giving me the orientation of what to do when I got there. I was taught about gardening and archery and all kinds of things and then began to workout, shaved my head and became a killer. Hell, I was there for years. I had over two hundred skulls on poles as a warning. I could make a fucking booby trap with my eyes closed. Why do you think I can shoot so well? I did it! I even killed those annoying reporters they sent me. Do you know who my first kill was?"

"Who? Please tell us," they all chimed in leaning toward him.

"Duncan Tess."

"Duncan Tess, the child rapist killer? That Duncan Tess?"

"The one."

"Okay this is really getting weird. Tell me, Donny, how did he die or how did you kill him?" asked Robert.

"Two booby traps. The first one I made with the leg bones from a beef carcass. They nailed him in each leg above his knees. The second one had nine spikes made from the ribs of the same carcass that hit him across the belly."

"Were the wounds like these?" asked the sergeant showing him the phone. "These are the pictures of Tess's autopsy. Notice the nine puncture marks in the exact places you said. Duncan Tess was killed in prison several years ago. Do you remember any of the other inmates you killed?"

Don then took a pen and paper and wrote down the ones he remembered which was a rather lengthy list and with each one, his friend, his trainer showed him how they had died including the two journalists who had died in a riot but Don knew otherwise.

"So it wasn't just a dream, was it?" he asked no one in particular.

"Apparently not. I've heard of these in ancient legends but never thought they existed. You made them happen," mentioned the new instructor.

"That's why I can do these things so well. I'm a killer, aren't I?" he began to sob as his wife and best friend Robert attempted to comfort him.

"Okay, Don, this is what's going to happen. We are going to intensify your training but tomorrow you and your wife are going to each get a pet."

Chapter 4

Just after dinner, some searches were made and low and behold, there was one place within five miles of the compound that took in abandoned or injured wild animals, cared for them and either sent them to zoos or released them into the wild. When the call was made by Robert there had been a newborn female puma cub that was found that day which couldn't have been more than a couple of days old. It was being nursed by a mother cat that had just given birth to a litter herself. An arrangement was made that the mother and her young would come to live with the Trumps until the cub was sufficiently weaned at which time the other cats would be given good homes. Under normal circumstances, a baby puma would have zero chance of surviving in the wild even if in good condition because it would have no knowledge of survival skills. It would also be illegal to have one as a pet but this was a different situation altogether so no laws would be broken. There was another place nearby that raised and sold llamas and some crias or babies had just been weaned. The first lady would go and not just pick out the one she wanted but allow them to approach her to decide which was decided to be the best way. Naturally, she would go there incognito and once, preferably a female was chosen it would be delivered. The puma, on the other hand was to be picked up by Martha the cook and Ho while bringing a substantial cash donation in the form of several large stacks of new bills. Documents provided by the State Game and Fish Commission indicating the situation making it completely legal.

"Don, are you ready to make a donation to the animal rescue place?" the sergeant asked while entering the fitness area as he was being instructed by Ho.

"Couple of hundred grand in my upper right hand desk drawer. Help yourself," came the nonchalant reply.

Don didn't come to bed that night but instead spent the entire night focusing energy and by morning had learned to move a few objects at will.

"I feel like a Jedi," he said as the sun began to rise.

"You are definitely not what I expected," remarked Ho.

"Hell, I'm not what I expected. How did this happen?"

"Some things are best left to be unknown. What I do know is that you will need these abilities."

"But why do I need a pet, a cat and a big one on top of that why is it the same with my wife?"

It was explained to Don that he needed balance in his life and something more to care for, something not human but not common either. He needed something to draw attention away from himself. Certainly he loved his wife more now than ever before and loved his son and other children but none of them really needed him. An animal, a pet such as this needed not only is care to survive but his caring, his love in a different way. Don had grown in so many ways and simply accepted this. He recalled when he first met his new mentor not to question his motives or orders and apologized sincerely.

"You know best," he said holding his head low in shame.

"It's okay. I know this is an odd situation but you are changing. This I feel will expedite it even more. Don, you are like a movie I once saw in which a very ugly character told his new friend that he was like an onion with many layers. Your layers are being discarded to reveal the real you."

It seemed like during every session of exercise due to the coaching of Ho, Don changed and increased his power. Even when he began lifting weights, they became lighter and lighter partially due to his physical strength but also due to the power he was developing. Outside he realized he could move a car or anything for that matter and also propel various objects at targets with deadly accuracy and force but at the same time had become a more likeable and gentle man.

At the appointed time, one in one direction while the second in another. Picking up the puma and other cats was a simple matter yet with the llama it was different. As Mrs. Trump entered the compound or farm, almost the very minute she left the large black SUV, a small llama came up to her and began nuzzling her immediately. There was an immediate bond.

"Sorry ma'am," apologized the young teen, a cute girl of around high school age who began putting leash around the neck of the young animal.

"Oh no, that's fine," responded the first lady.

"Never seen one take to a stranger like that especially one that has recently been taken away from her mother."

"I'll take her," came the response as the small llama continued to try and show affection to the stranger wearing sunglasses and a large floppy hat.

"I can't help it but you look familiar."

"People are always telling me that," she laughed as she continued to pet the young one.

It was decided that the baby llama would be loaded into a special van designed for transporting both young and old and the first lady told the owner that she wanted to ride with it to the house. Naturally, two agents were to accompany her on the short journey. Within less than fifteen minutes, payment had been made along with the necessary papers of ownership and inoculations and then they were on their way. In the meantime when the cats were brought by Martha and Ho, Don was there displaying uncharacteristic excitement.

"I don't think I've ever had a pet before and now I'm getting a lion? What a way to start!" he beamed.

The mother cat was a friendly sort. Typical yellow striped tabby who was constantly licking each baby and made no distinction between her own and the newest one which was at that time the same size as the others yet was soon to change. There were seven identical kittens all like their mother plus one smoky grey and brown with black spots in an irregular pattern. Don made sure to avoid touching them and they were initially placed in the kitchen were the mother was given a choice of canned tuna, fresh salmon and regular cat food along with a bowl of water. Each item was tested at which she looked up for some sort of approval from the humans who only smiled. The name the center had given her was Mama which suited her and the first name that came to mind from Don for his new "child" was Baby, a name that fit the cat.

"When people hear old Donny has a cat and one named Baby, won't they be surprised when they meet it especially after it's all matured?" he laughed.

After about a week, the kittens had begun moving more and Don felt it was alright to handle his which had grown to more than twice the size of the others. He could sense the surrogate mother's approval and even though its eyes were not open yet, the little one was aware of him and began to nuzzle his fingers and face as he held it and gave it a bottle with a special formula advised by the veterinarian who worked with the center. Dolly the llama was a good companion for the wife and was her constant shadow and she worked in the garden often being given treats along with hugs and soft talk. The animal was allowed in the house and never used any spot except for a box outside to eliminate; basically she was housebroken. The specialist had told them it would be the same with the cat and since they were basically being raised together they would look at themselves as the same species instead of predator and prey.

Chapter 5

With two additions to the household came more joy. Even though Baby's eyes had not yet opened, she could tell when Don was nearby and seemed to love when Dolly came to visit. They were all bonding yet at the same time, Don, himself was expanding his mind through the training of Ho. He had nearly advanced as far as he could physically so that part was being gradually reduced as the other took over. Robert found a gun shop in the area that had a nice range and began to schedule some sessions after hours with the owner who had retired from the service and was a good friend and also knew it best to ask few if any questions. Ho, however had another form of training, one that would advance his student's mind beyond anything he could ever conceive.

What began as a simple guided meditation ended up being more than what student or teacher could have imagined in their wildest dreams.

"Don, I want you to imagine yourself in a library. Any type will do but just get it in your mind," he began.

"Okay, I can see it. Huge bookcases loaded to the ceiling with all kinds of books. I can hardly see the top. Millions of them! I can even smell the place!" he said with his eyes firmly closed.

"Good. Now I want you to select a few and take them to a table and begin reading them. You can touch them and know every single word. It is like you can transfer the thought that have been written down directly into your brain. What are you studying?"

"Law. I am studying American law. It's the United States Constitution. I know it! Now I am looking at American history. There's a book on presidents. I know them all. More books. So much to learn."

"Continue studying, reading. If you like, you can go to another library and find more books."

This exercise went on for hours and finally by time for lunch he was called out of it.

"I understand more than I could have ever known," Don said to his friend Robert.

"You studied the Constitution?"

"Yes, many books on it. Could you ask me a question or twenty?"

Robert began with the basics and as each question was answered correctly, he moved up level after level after level until he realized he could go no higher. Then he started asking questions on history, politics and other related topics with perfect answers to all of the questions asked.

"Don, you sound like some of my professors. I now wonder if you could pass the Bar exam? You learned all this in a few hours?"

"Yes, it's so simple. It was like I could look at a book even a very thick one and know the entire contents with a feel. Weird, huh?"

After the meal, even though the student wanted to go back to the books in his mind and at the libraries he wished to visit, it was decided he needed to become familiar with firearms so he and Robert went about ten miles down the road to his friend Larry who owned the gun shop and range. The store had been closed with a sign telling customers it was being renovated for the afternoon yet would be open at another time.

When they entered, the former agent knew exactly who his new client was.

"Mr. President," he began, "It's an honor to meet you. Larry Young."

"It's Don or Donny, Mr. Young."

"Very well, Don. It's Larry; I want you to browse and pick out what you are drawn to. Ask me any questions you like."

Within less than ten minutes several selections had been made.

"I don't think I have ever held a gun in my life even though I told people I had a license but that was one of my many lies. Still, these got my attention. I love the feel of them especially the Italian make. The one made in Austria is popular but seems a bit boxy. The other feels good in my hand. Does that make any sense?"

"Sounds like when Harry Potter was at the wand shop where he was told that the wand chose the wizard. Guess we need to see how it feels to fire the weapon."

Don was instructed on the safety of handgun which was first and foremost before he began to fire it at some paper targets only ten feet away. When he did fire, the first shot was dead center followed by the second, third and entire magazine. It was as if he had only fired once. The targets were then moved to greater distances and met with similar results.

"Mr. President, uh sorry I mean Don, you said you had never fired a gun before or don't believe you have even held one but you don't miss. How is that possible?"

"Beats me. You know, we have a large place and do you know anyone who can build a shooting range, an indoor one not just for guns but for archery as well. I had a trainer from Alabama who taught me that."

"I know the guy. Second best in the world from what I hear. I will set it up with a friend of mine who can build you what you want."

The outing was good and when they left, eight weapons had been purchased, four for him and four for Robert. As he carried two of the Italian models under each armpit, he loved the feel. The other two were a bit larger but for some reason he was drawn to them. When they got home, it was still only a little after midday and dinner was a long way off so it was decided to get with Ho once more for another session at the libraries. The wife loved how the guns looked on her husband and commented that they made him look like a "real badass." Before the exercise, however he felt a need to cradle Baby for a while who he could tell had missed him in her own blind way. Her eyes were just becoming small blue slits but he could tell she recognize this man who did love her. She had begun sucking on his fingers and also he had started feeding her massed up fish with milk as instructed by the wild animal experts. Then he placed her back with the others who were sleeping having nursed and soon she was in the same state.

Chapter 6

Don continued visiting the libraries going through stacks and stacks of hundreds and thousands of books over the course of the next few days. He even went through some in other countries and began conversing in Chinese with Robert and in Japanese with Ho. Since the sergeant had studied law, just for fun, they got a copy of the Bar Exam simply to see how much the former president had actually retained. After about twenty minutes, Don put down his pencil.

"Something wrong?" asked his friend.

"No. I've finished. How long is this supposed to take?"

"Hours. You did it in twenty minutes. How do you think you did?"

"Seemed easy."

"Well, let's see if it was as you thought."

It took more than thirty minutes to grade the test. It wasn't a perfect score because one question was missed. It wasn't actually missed. It was just not answered. Everything else, though was spot on.

"Oh hell, I knew that one!" said the student slapping himself in the head.

"Okay, what next? Are you going to pass the medical boards and become a surgeon? I have got to schedule some time with Ho."

"Join us. The more the merrier."

The training continued as did the testing and soon the shooting and indoor archery range was completed but also, Baby's eyes had opened and she was becoming a playful kitten while eating solid food often lapping it from her "daddy's" hand. She purred like a normal cat although a bit louder and the others loved her but soon realized it was time for them to leave and the larger animal seemed to understand. Now she had her own family and was happy. After she was thoroughly weaned, she became independent yet never left the compound on her own. For the most part, if she wasn't with Don, she was with Dolly who she loved and the love was returned. The cat had gotten to where she had developed a love of certain vegetables including the smaller or cherry tomatoes, leaf lettuce and green beans. Perhaps it was due to her best friend, Dolly but regardless, it was good thing to have these additions to her diet. Even though after several months, she had developed sharp claws, she never tested them on the furniture but had a post outside which she was instinctively drawn to and knew its purpose.

Baby, despite what she was, an apex predator, was a docile feline who loved attention and affection and sought it from anyone especially Don. The other agents who initially considered the assignment more of a punishment detail having been assured it was temporary discovered it to be the best they could imagine. In many ways they were pampered. Often either Don or his wife would bring them various foods and other gifts and when it was found they were having family problems were allowed to take as much time off as needed or when there was a sick child or other issue, funds happened to appear along with the best doctors, therapists and the like. Instead of an arrogant boss, Donald Trump or this Trump turned out to be totally different. He was warm, kind and humorous who treated them as equals much to their surprise. The man still had money but nothing on the scope as before and during this time, it was of low significance.

The agents had thought that most of their time would be spent at the golf course or attending rambunctious rallies composed of screaming brainless followers who would believe anything from someone who would naturally assure them that he would indeed return or rise again as the old Confederacy had once decreed. Instead, he spent most of his time training in some fashion and after having the range built even saw no need to leave the compound at all. He even invited them, the guards to dine with him and had a fine barbeque area placed where they lived often surprising them with items that they craved such as fresh seafood, steaks of every type and always kept mental notes of each agent's preferences. The former president was found as time went on to be a quiet man who listened more than spoke and everyone was happy about the change especially the wife who at one time had planned on divorcing him yet now it was obvious that she had fallen deeply in love with the man she had married.

As Don continued with his training mostly from Ho, an even greater transformation occurred in the fact that after one such outings in his mental exercises, it became apparent that he could communicate with animals. After nearly a full day in his trance-like state, upon opening his eyes, he began a series of yips and low growls directed toward the cat sitting at his feet as similar sounds were returned.

"You really loved your sister, didn't you Ho?" he asked looking up.

"Yes, but how did you know? I haven't spoken to you or anyone about her in years."

"You sometimes talk to yourself and cry when you are alone or think you are," Don confided in a matter of fact manner.

"Yes but…how?" I mean how could you know this?"

"Baby told me. She goes walking with you sometimes at night, doesn't she?"

"You don't mean to tell me that you speak Puma, do you?"

"Your parents only had two children and you were the youngest. They were killed in a plane crash when you weren't even a teen and you had to live with relatives. Your sister's name was Keiko who died along with the baby during childbirth."

"A puma told you this. Baby told you, right?"

"Yes. I guess I do know their language and it seems that most animals have a spoken one."

Through the exercise, the knowledge of the universe came to the former president even to the point to where he could see the future. One night during dinner as Don was cooking having given Martha some time off, he began to talk while sending plates to the table without touching them which is something his closest friends began to expect, he started a conversation.

"It's time for me to get back into politics," he began.

"Honey, I was wondering when you would make that decision," his wife responded first.

"Yes, my love, I think I need to make up for my previous transgressions. Also I think there are certain things that I can do better than the current administration. Definitely have got to get rid of those stupid political parties. They do more harm than good. There's going to be another pandemic worse than the one before and nobody is even planning for it. I also want you, Robert to be my running mate but not just second fiddle but more of a co-president. Will you accept the role?"

"Gladly, sir."

"Okay, let's set it up and start the thing moving."

Part 3

Chapter I

It had been three years almost to the day since anyone had seen or heard of former President Donald John Trump, the forty-fifth president of the United States. It was then that he allowed the major networks to come to his residence in northern Florida where he said he had a major announcement. This stirred up everything with all kinds of speculations since the former chief executive had not even been seen in all that time. There had been no messages on social media and was as if he had become a hermit. His office had declined interviews and all rallies had been cancelled. Offers of speaking engagements with the high price tags associated with them had been declined as well plus he had not written a single page of a memoir as common of most former leaders. People still donated to his website and there was well over half a billion untouched dollars accumulating interest in it. There were the hats and t-shirts and banners, pictures and such but a management company dealt with all that and merely added the funds to the account while taking their cut. The odd thing also was that no presidential library had even been planned. It was as if Donald J. Trump had dropped off the face of the planet but now after three years he wanted to talk.

After the reporters had been screened by security along with the photographers, they were escorted into the garden area where vegetables and flowers were growing in abundance. At that moment a large bald man appearing to be in his late thirties or early forties approached wearing perfectly pressed khaki pants, running shoes and a pull over name brand green sports shirt displaying his massive physique including muscles on top of muscles walked up to a podium and began to speak. From his appearance he looked like the winner of the Mr. Universe Bodybuilding Championship. He was flanked on one side by another equally massive bald black man and the easily-recognizable former first lady. At that moment he began to speak but was interrupted within less than thirty seconds.

"Ladies and gentlemen. I wanted to thank you for coming at such short..."

"Excuse me sir, we were told that Donald Trump was to meet us here. We see his wife but when will President Trump arrive?"

"In answer to your question, you're looking at him. I am Donald John Trump. Don't you recognize me or at least my voice? I'll tell you what, rather than just pick one of you for each question, why not stick with the same reporter for now, okay? Does it really matter who asks the question or are you guys paid on commission? After all, I did invite you, right? Please continue."

"You are President Donald Trump? What happened to the hair and belly?"

"Okay, first of all, thanks for the questions. The focus with the hair was getting old and everyone wondered if it was real. The color wasn't but hair was and I got tired of it and also my diet sucked and had a shitty exercise routine. Come on, golf? That's not exercise. One of the most boring games on the planet and also, for the love of God, please do not call me President Trump. That title is reserved for those who deserve it. I was an awful president and you all know it. That's a title of respect so give it to those who have earned it like President Biden, Obama and others. My name is Don or Donny so none of this Mr. President bullshit. If you need to see my fingerprints or get a DNA sample, I will provide them. That's my wife as you can see and my good friend Sergeant Robert Sims. Oh and we have a pet now or two pets to be exact. A cat which is mine that came from an animal rescue center and we think its mother either abandoned it or was killed but we decided to adopt it. Her name is Baby. Care to meet her?"

"Yes, Mister…"

"What did I say about that Mister shit? It's Don or Donny."

"Very well, Donny. Sure we would love to meet your cat," replied the young reporter.

"Baby. Where are you? Here kitty, kitty, kitty," nearly sang the former president.

In less than ten seconds, Baby appeared and leaped into Don's arms nearly knocking him down while licking his face causing everyone seated to jump with some screaming.

"Calm down. Baby's a good girl. A great cat. Trust me, she doesn't have a problem with dogs. In fact, she may chase them. Oh my wife has a pet, too," he announced, "and no, it's not another cat."

The former first lady called for Dolly and the llama appeared humming and rubbing her face and doing the same to the large feline who returned the favor even going between its legs like a normal house cat might do yet due to the size with some difficulty. It was easy to tell they were best of friends.

"Come on guys. It's just a cat and a llama and some bald headed bozo that you guys used to hate and probably still do. Okay, enough of the family meeting stuff. You are here because I want to announce my candidacy for president of the United States…again. Let me save you at least one question and would hope that you would be respectful and not interrupt. I know you learned that behavior from me but let's do some unlearning, okay? Why am I running you ask? Perhaps to get it right this time. The current president and vice president are doing a hell of a job but I feel I should be able to do better. Maybe I learned from my mistakes. Maybe I'm growing up. If I'm elected, fine. If not I gave it my best shot and also I'm going to do something very different that instead of waiting until the convention if I make it that far to announce my choice of my running mate, the man you see to my right Robert Adam Sims here. Harvard educated lawyer who spent ten years in the Army and was a member of the United States Secret Service. He has nothing to hide unlike what I was always trying to do. Now you can ask your questions."

"Sir, have you found religion or something like that?" asked another reporter.

"I like that question and expected it. Let me ask you a question. Do you have to find religion? Do you?"

"Well, uh, uh…"

"Okay, sorry to interrupt but isn't religion always there? It's a tool and do you really need a book to tell you something you should naturally be and that is good? No. Do you really need people to tell you what a book means? I never was a good Christian and only used it to get votes. I used to call you guys fake news but I was the real fake. The hair, the ego all that nonsense. I don't think that I have earned any sort of salvation if there is any. I believe in God and all that but I am happy without any formal religion. Can you prove God exists? No. Can you prove God does not exist? Of course not. If that costs me votes so be it but I'm going to be myself perhaps for the first time. Hell, I told over twenty-three thousand lies during my term as president according to you guys and a lot of them I believed. Now it's time to tell the truth. I don't mind you asking questions but picking fights will only make you look bad. Opinionated journalism is not reporting but if you guys want to play those games, all it's going to do is embarrass you when the tapes are played back but that's up to you. I know that when you all go back home to your offices and studios and try and make me look bad can you make me look any worse than I made myself look during my four years as president? Go ahead and doubt my sincerity and hope to get a response out of me but you will only be wasting your time. I always thought reporters were supposed to report and isn't that telling others what they see? If you're going to make up some story, why even go to the scene? Go ahead and go for the ratings if that's what you want yet never tell someone you are a reporter."

"Sir, you've been pretty much out of the loop for three years. No memoirs, no library, no rallies, none of those high-paid speeches, why?"

"Come on, a Donald Trump Presidential Library? Where would it be, in the corner of some Walmart between automotive and the pet department? Oh yeah, clean up on isle one; a book fell. What the hell did I accomplish? All I did was piss people off and made myself look like a bigger idiot than I already was. I needed to look at myself and when I did, I didn't like who and what I saw. Do I like myself now? I like what I am becoming if that makes any sense but go ahead and write your crap for ratings and I'm okay with that. Try and get a rise out of me. It won't be as easy this time. I do want you guys to spend the day with me though. Stay as long as you like. Why do you think one of the stipulations of you people coming was to bring a bag with at least three days of clothing? We'll have a drawing and let three of you spend a week or so with me. There's a washing machine here but if you need more clothes we can always buy some. They say there's a department store up the road from what I hear.

We'll put your business cards in a hat and myself or Sergeant Sims will pick three of you to stick around for a while. How's that? Those selected will have pretty much free reign of the place except for the bedroom. There may be times when I need to have some private meetings with Robert and Mr. Ho there but I will let you know when I am not available but aside from those times, you guys can follow me and Baby around as much as you like. Agreed?"

More questions were asked and notebooks were passed out detailing the candidate's agenda. Everything was in black and white and clearly outlined.

"As you can see, everything is written clearly. If you wish to distort it, I will call you out on it. No, I will not call lawyers nor will I sue. I will instead embarrass you by telling the truth and let you be the ones lying. Hell of a twist, isn't it?"

"Sir, what party will you be affiliated with?" asked another reporter who was known to be quite annoying.

"Personally I would rather not be affiliated with any party to be honest with you. The Democrats have some very strong candidates or one in particular so no point in watering down that group so I guess I will stick with the Republicans but sure as hell wish that people would vote for the person. Both parties have great ideas but they tend to spend time fighting each other just because they are of a different affiliation. Kind of like a race war. Look, I'm not trying to get the black votes or evangelicals or any of those because if anyone says they want a certain group, it makes them a racist, doesn't it? Vote for me because you want to, not because of some damned party."

"But sir, your running mate is black."

"No fucking shit, Sherlock. You don't miss a thing, do you? Look, Sergeant Sims is probably my best friend and I trust him. He served his country, is a Harvard law school graduate, speaks three Asian languages oh and you're telling me he is black? The man's got credentials out the ass and you are focusing on his skin color? What a narrow-minded prick you are. You're the racist for bringing up all that crap. Everyone is racist or prejudice to some degree, aren't they? You guys think about this. Some of you don't believe I am actually Donald John Trump. I'm going to prove it to you. See that van over there? The one that says American Red Cross on it. Okay, they are going to take my blood and do a DNA test while you wait. They will also test for drugs and all kinds of things and give you each a report. My fingerprints will be taken by those FBI agents over there and sent to their database in which my DNA is also housed. While we're waiting, everyone can come in the house while I rustle up some food. I've got some good steaks and lobsters. Plenty for everyone. Baby has hers rare and Dolly likes salads which came from the garden. While everything's cooking, I need to pump some iron and you guys can join me or watch. Up to you. We're not formal here. Got some appetizers set up in the fitness area. Nothing fancy but most of it I made myself. Got a nice smoker out back."

As the steaks were grilling and other items being prepared, the former president removed his shirt and began with right at three hundred pounds on the bench for thirty reps and then finally maxing out at five hundred for ten just to show the group the change. He had a well-defined physique along with a perfect six pack regarding his abs. Robert, naturally was spotting him, yelling a string of profanities encouraging the former president to push even harder. They knew that some of the male reporters doubted the weights and were told they could test them for themselves. Some found out the hard way that they were indeed real. Don even did a few curls with some dumbbells that exceeded one hundred pounds. Then he did something quite remarkable and that was to get a stronger bar and load it with more weights than anyone had ever seen which was just shy of half a ton. Little did they know that he was using the powers that he had learned and did nearly a dozen perfect reps.

"Not bad for an old man, eh? I think President Biden once tried to challenge me to a push up contest. I don't think he could bench this kind of weight. Kind of surprised I can but like anything, it's a gradual thing. Oh, and ladies, gentlemen, the tests will indicate that I do not have any drugs in my system. Never saw the need and Sergeant Sims has also been my trainer and saw to that and a healthy lifestyle so come on guys don't lie to the public. There was enough of that when I was president but no more. Mr. Ho, here teaches me to focus and between the two of them I'm getting pretty balanced. It's always nice, though to have an animal my other best friend, Baby with me so whenever I go, she goes. Feel free to pet her. She's a good cat. A bit large but she has a large heart along with her size."

The meal was perfect and casual and everyone was surprised that the former president did some of the cooking and cleaning plus how devoted he was to the large cat and his wife. His voice had even changed to one of a less pompous tone and wasn't all about himself. He mentioned the problems in America and felt between him and Robert how they felt they could fix them but mostly emphasized that with the right team, they could help a lot of people.

"Look, Robert knows the Constitution backwards and forward and if I don't know something which is a lot, I'm not going to bullshit you but instead tell you I don't know and refer you to him or someone else. I know you guys get off on digging up all kinds of dirt on everyone and in doing so gives you a sense of power and is a way of making up for your own sexual inadequacies. Digging up stuff on me is easy due to the trials and all the stuff I pulled but if you go after my running mate, you won't find shit. Quote

Alcatraz Awaits: The Legacy of Donald Trump

me on all that. If you guys don't like my language, then at the next press conference, stay home and make up some stupid story and sell it to the tabloids. I'll curb it when necessary but for the most part it's going to be in ways you guys understand and that's blunt and dirty. Remember a guy named Harry Truman? Well, I'm not going to insult the man by comparing myself to him but didn't he pretty well speak in this tone?"

Pictures were taken and the analysis of the blood and fingerprints came back as expected. It was indeed Donald John Trump. At that they all went their separate ways with the exception of the three chosen.

Turning to his staff and wife, he remarked, "I think that went well, don't you guys?"

Cheers and hugs began and continued for several minutes.

The reporters had been ushered to their rooms yet opted to venture out to hopefully hear something that they thought might be opposite of what they had been told.

"You know, I like these people," began the former president. "One of them, as I recall used to give me all kinds of shit but he seems okay. Actually, I'm kind of glad they are here. You know, if I'm elected, a couple of them might be good candidates for press secretary. Nice to have visitors. Robert, Ho, we are behind in our training, aren't we? Treadmill? You know, another thing I just thought of. The current president has some pretty good members of the cabinet. Why get rid of someone that's qualified and is doing a good job? I don't give a shit if they are Democrats or anything. Fuck that partisan shit."

"Are you hearing this?" asked one of the reporters listening nearby.

"Yeah, I never thought I would hear that from this one or anyone. You did record that, didn't you? Tell me you did, Sarah," asked the second.

"Every word."

Back in the kitchen it was different.

"Yes Donny. You really need to sweat out that meal," mentioned Robert.

"Good idea. What do you think, level ninety-nine? Let's max it out. Let me get rid of this damned monkey suit. Baby, ready for a run? Honey, why not ask our guests if they want to come to the gym or what are your plans?"

"Orchids need attending and I thought I would work in the garden for a while."

"Okay, maybe one or two can help you. Martha, how about surprising us with some of your magic in the kitchen. If you need anything you know who to ask. Looks like I've got at least four or five hours ahead of me in the gym. Thanks."

The reporters for the sake of referring to them as only "reporters" named Sam, Sarah and Glen were an interesting bunch. They were hungry to make names for themselves and were elated that they had been chosen for this assignment. They were thrilled even more when they were chosen to spend a week with this man the former president of the United States who they had known was a self-centered egomaniac. What they heard, though was not what they wanted. They wanted to meet and get a rise out of Donald Trump, not a cross between Gandhi and The Terminator. Never had they seen anyone change as much as this one man. However, being reporters, they knew there had to be something hidden under the profanity, muscles and humility. As he was working out, there were occasions when he would lapse into speaking Japanese to the mysterious Mr. Ho often laughing and then rattling off in Chinese with Robert and then even a series of those odd yips and growls to the cat.

"Mister, I mean, uh Donny, you speak Japanese?" asked Sarah.

"Yeah, sure," he replied pushing over half a ton on the leg press.

"And Chinese?" asked Sam.

"Yes, so? Goddammit Robert! You fucking slave driver. I did thirty reps!" he shouted while doing two more.

"We didn't know you spoke those languages."

"Sometimes it helps to ask, doesn't it? If you guys weren't so busy trying find shit on everybody you might learn something. Ask questions without knowing the answers ahead of time or when you ask them, accept the answer. Don't keep on pushing until you get the one you want. What the fuck is wrong with you guys? Report, you bastards!" he continued to shout as he kept being pushed to the limits of his endurance.

"Tell you what, either tonight or tomorrow you guys can come to the archery range out back and try your hand at shooting."

"You're an archer, sir?" asked Glenn.

"I dabble in it. Keeps my head clear."

"Dabble my ass," chimed the sergeant.

"Oh come on Robert. I'm not that good."

"The hell you aren't. You mean that hitting a Coke can in the air at one hundred yards isn't good?"

"Lucky shot, that's all it was."

"You call ten in a row, lucky?"

"Okay, ten lucky shots. Are you happy?"

"So typical of good ole Donny…"

"Sorry guys. I wish now that I had never even heard of the game of golf. Such a grand waste of time and real estate. I'm actually glad I had all of those problems and had to sell those courses. Fucking snobatoriums."

"Now wait a minute Donny. You and I both know that you do like golf to some degree. What about the times after you were first trained by that expert from Alabama."

"Oh, I had forgotten about that," Don mentioned.
"Folks, uh do you want to tell this or can I?" asked Robert.
"Hey, go for it buddy."
"Okay, he wanted to learn how to hit moving targets and was doing pretty well but then he came up with this completely insane idea of going to a local golf course and just for the hell of it, stood off in the uh, what do they call those places on either side of the fairway?"
"Rough," mentioned one of the reporters.
"Yeah, that's it, rough. Anyway, Donny stands there where nobody can see him about forty yards away from the tee. We are behind him and these guys come up and tee off. Well, what does this idiot do? You guessed it. He starts shooting the balls as they are driven. Missed a few at first but then got the hang of it and after that it was one after another and he was using broad-heads like you would hunt big game with. Oh and it gets better. We went off to the side also hidden at the green and there's this guy putting. The ball's about to go into the hole and Don's up in a tree maybe thirty yards away and the arrow keeps the ball from going in. Poor fellow. Started running like hell thinking he was being attacked by Indians! Don is deadly. Don't let him bullshit you."
"Good teachers," came the reply in a low more like humble tone.
"Got to expect replies like that."
Conversations went on like this at all hours and during the course of the week they were with the former president, the more they grew to like and admire him. There were even privy to discussions of the United States Constitution and when they were discussing it, it wasn't just Robert that could quote parts pertinent to the discussion but Don himself line by line. Even when the subject of religion came up, they found that he had

apparently memorized the entire Bible and offered to let them test him by randomly selecting a book, chapter and verse which he knew word for word but chalked it up as merely guessing. This was not the same person that they and everyone else had known during those tumultuous four years but someone who should now be the leader of the nation. It wasn't like the others in power were bad but this one, this new Donald Trump was so much more refined and likeable. This was not only evident in how he was in the kitchen, the fitness or shooting ranges but how he related to the large cat, the puma who was constantly at his side and it could tell how much it was loved. It was the same with the llama and naturally the wife.

The night before Sarah, Sam and Glenn were to leave after a little more than a week, they realized they really didn't want to go home. Don, Robert and Ho along with the first lady had discovered these were genuinely good people so it had been discussed to offer them jobs helping with the campaign. At the table they were told that they would be paid a considerable amount more than their current salaries and if he was elected president, would all have positions as press secretaries and the like.

"In your contracts, you will see that it clearly states your salary and these positions on the premise that if I am elected. Take it to your attorneys and this way you will not be screwed over but if you want to work for me now just let me know when you can start."

Each one knew this was too good to be true and within two weeks they were onboard.

Chapter 2

Donald Trump needed the press and they needed him. One of the three he had hired had been a royal pain to him for four years as he was crude and deceitful must like himself but now he was warned not to play a dirty game with the others. He let them know that regardless of what the other candidates did, there would be no dirty politics. There would be no name calling, no insults or any other thing like in the past. If they wanted to play those games, he would not respond. However, if any candidate made any false claims against him, he expected them to be called out and prove what they had said with actual evidence. The idea of a clean election or campaign was practically foreign to the press or even the candidates but his people had their orders.

"My campaign will be a clean one. If you tarnish it, I will fire you. Don't test me," he pointed out and they knew he was serious. "I will not have you worried about your jobs or whether one day you would have one and the next not but I just want to lay all the cards on the table from the first day and you will know the rules and what's expected of you. Since in our nation we have a system of checks and balances, I expect each of you to exercise this with each other. Kind of stupid of me to have to manage you guys and I think that you can deal with your own issues. Anything you can't handle, you come to me. Any ideas you have, either discuss them with each other or come to me."

The way of getting the word out would be mostly the internet yet there were some talk shows that jumped at the chance of bringing him on as a guest especially after what the others had reported. One stipulation was that he would never be alone and would at least have Baby with him. During one kids' show, he allowed children to come and pet the large animal who proved to be as kind as any lazy house cat that was seen in millions of households in the country. It even tried to get in the former president's lap which wasn't the easiest thing and generated many laughs. It had a collar but no leash and responded to everything Don said. Other than that, Robert was there and people were also amazed that the former first lady was more talkative and had changed her Slavic accent to a more neutral tone and wore conservative attire that seemed to be more like that worn by the average American woman. Sometimes she was seen shopping at department stores or working in the garden or greenhouse with her orchids or in the kitchen helping the staff.

As who was coined as "the new Donald Trump" came into the public eye, initially his sincerity was doubted. Never did he hide his previous behavior and had admitted that he had been many things most of which could not be said in public and even told anyone who would listen that when he reflected on his life, he was embarrassed and felt that maybe in some ways if given another chance to hold this office or another one, might be a chance of redemption. He even blamed himself repeatedly for the pandemic which had surged due to his arrogance and stupidity during his administration. He gave absurd advice, ignored warnings, didn't take precautions while displaying no empathy to those of whom he was supposed to protect. Part of the reason he sought re-election was to correct the sins of the past, his past.

"Do you feel any sort of fear of an afterlife? What we mean is are you doing this to save your soul or avoid damnation?" asked a host of a Christian talk show.

"I don't know if there is an afterlife. For someone like me, I would hope not but for people like the current president and even yourself, I would hope there was. I mean, look at my past. Do I deserve forgiveness? No, of course not and would be a greater fool to even consider the thought. Why dwell in the future because it's unwritten or as it was said in the movie KUNG FU PANDA, the past is history, tomorrow a mystery but today is a gift; that's why it's called the present."

Interviews like this continued and even the staff that that had been recruited from the reporters let others know that the man they worked for was sincere.

"When we arrived at his home, we tried to find out how real he was and recorded some very secret conversations and there is no way he could be up to anything except the real deal. The man's an open book. What got into him during those three years of isolation was the best thing that could have happened to anyone. He never seems to get angry yet takes a lot of punishment from Sergeant Sims when he is working out. This Donald Trump is a very disciplined man, strong as hell yet as gentle as they come and very easy going. If we didn't know better, we would not know this was the same person who was president. This is a likeable person and we wanted to find as much dirt on him as we could but aside from his past, there is none. He has ordered us to run a clean campaign and there will be no negative ads. Maybe everyone needs some time alone but whatever happened, it happened for the good of one."

Alcatraz Awaits: The Legacy of Donald Trump

When there were gatherings, he made it a point to have lots of small ones instead of several large ones and they were quiet and respectful. If anyone shouted anything bad about another candidate, they were admonished or asked to leave. Never did he wear a coat and tie or put on any sort of airs. When he was critical, he was critical of himself and if his past was brought up by his adversaries, he simply asked them how many times was it necessary for these issues to be addressed.

"Do I have to be reminded of my transgressions constantly?" he asked. "I know I fucked up and what I did or didn't do haunts me constantly. I punish myself more than you, God or Satan ever could but if you get your jollies by reminding me and the public of these things go for it. Is that the best you can do? Look, we have a whole hell of a lot of more important issues to correct than trying to make me feel or look bad. Doesn't the Christian Bible in the book of John chapter 8 verse 7 say, "he who is without sin may he cast the first stone?"

"You know the Bible?" they would ask.

"I memorized it along with the Torah and Koran, the United States Constitution plus those of every major world power and feel free to test me on these. Can you quote any of these word for word? Perhaps it would help if we were familiar with the laws of our adversaries. Can you recite the Declaration of Independence, our constitution or that of the Chinese for that matter, in Chinese? If you can't why are you trying to be the leader of the free world?"

When the public heard this and saw it proven, they saw it proven that this was the person they needed to run the country. This new Donald Trump was a leader the likes the nation has always wanted. He was no longer the bully, the egomaniac, the spoiled rich kid.

Another odd thing was that he often invited the other candidates to his home for casual talk and simple meals at which they got to meet the family and his staff. During one such visit, he told the current president that if the election went in his favor defeating the incumbent, he didn't see the need in replacing several members of his cabinet since they were good at their jobs and wouldn't mind staying on.

"Are you telling me, Mister, I mean Donny that if you defeat me in the election, you would not wipe the slate clean of my people?" asked the president.

"What's the point? You've got some good ones including the Secretary of State and a couple of others that are fine and I like them. If they want to leave though, it's entirely up to them but why start over? Just because a new coach comes in why replace the whole team?"

"But they are Democrats," the president added.

"Oh come on. I hate this fucking partisan shit! Pardon my language but all that does is divide. Now this may cause me to lose the election but if I am elected president, one of the first things I will do is abolish all political parties. They cause nothing but trouble and most people don't even know why they are affiliated with one or another anymore than what a democracy is or what socialism or communism is for that matter. America is a mixed economy for God's sake. George Washington didn't want political parties but he was voted down. Vote for the person not the damned party. Make sure you guys have what I said down because I said it and don't distort it. Report exactly what I said, not what you think I said or meant."

Instead of what Donald Trump said, having an adverse effect on his poll ratings, it did just the opposite. He surged in popularity. Animal rights people loved him because he had taken in a helpless puma cub that could have never survived in the wild and others loved him because he was open and honest and hid nothing. He didn't hold rallies but more like tailgate parties. During the debates, he never once interrupted the other candidates even allowing one to go over the time limit because he said he was enjoying what they had to say. However when he did speak, everyone listened. He insisted on being called Don or Donny and often Baby would sit at his feet and sleep. It soon became apparent that the election was to be a landslide in his favor and when all the votes were counted, it was even more so having won every state by huge margins.

Chapter 3

As the transition of power took place, he met with the outgoing president's staff including and especially the Cabinet asking if nearly half would remain under his administration which most gladly accepted. He even asked the outgoing president and vice president if they were interested in holding certain advisory positions which they both were happy to oblige.

"Look, I need you guys. I'm not the smartest person on the planet. Even if I have to create positions for you, I will do so."

Having members of the previous administration as advisors was unheard of even though most opted not to remain whereas the rest were asked to leave only because Don felt others were more suited yet these were placed in other areas such as ambassadors to various countries. The members of the press that worked with him were kept on as promised. One of the other promises he had made was the abolition all political parties and an executive order written the very afternoon after the swearing in ceremony. Initially there was some confusion but it wasn't long before this was accepted. There were parties naturally yet he only made brief appearances as he was busy at his desk getting back to work. This was another thing that confused the press corps and that was of a United States president who immediately got to work. He never even felt the need to redecorate the office.

"Where's the president?" they asked.

"In his office," came the reply from his chief of staff.

"Doing what?"

"His job. Working. You know, the thing he was elected to do."

"When will he attend the parties?"

"He won't."

"Why?" they persisted.

"He has work to do. The only reason myself and the others are here is because of our orders. We were also told to remind members of Congress to be at work first thing in the morning which means early. That's seven o'clock. Breakfast for the leaders is at 5:30. If any are absent, they have been told that the Secret Service will fetch them."

"Oh, there's one of them now. Need to remind him. Got to go."

As Sarah the former reporter left the other reporter, one of her former colleges who had been assigned to cover the festivities, she approached the senior senator who had been told when to report to the president.

"Uh, Senator, you realize that you and the other leaders are to have breakfast with the president at 5:30, don't you?" she began.

"Oh come on, uh Ms…"

"It's Sarah, the president's press secretary."

"Uh, yeah, uh Sarah. Come on, it's Inauguration Day. Lighten up. This shit can wait. Tell the president I'll see him when I see him. Here, have a drink."

"Senator, the president said if you are not there on time and I quote, he will have your lazy ass dragged out of bed and escorted to your destination dressed or not dressed, end of quote. Do you really want to test him? Now he can have Baby bring you but that will be by the scuff of the neck. Your call."

"Look young lady, you can't threaten me. I'm a United States senator!" he practically shouted.

"Sir, I didn't threaten you. All I did was pass along a message but you will attend as ordered."

Sarah did make a call to the president who soon appeared on a large screen in several of the banquet areas and on it was not only his image but also of many of the senators and congressmen being sworn in. the primary words emphasized were "to serve the American people" and "to the best of my ability."

"Ladies, gentlemen, senators and members of Congress. You saw and heard the oath that all of you swore especially the last part about to the best of your abilities. I expect you to fulfil this promise. As you can see, I am in my office doing something called work and I expect you guys to do the same. Do not embarrass yourselves. I will see a number of you at 5:30 and you know the place. Don't make me have to send some very large men and women to come and get you. I suggest you get to bed early. Trump out."

The video ended and soon for the most part the festivities also came to a conclusion. One of the leaders approached another member of Don's press staff, the one named Sam trying to excuse himself from the early morning meal and meeting but it was in vain. He was even allowed a video call to the president himself and was told that he would be there on his own volition or he would come kicking and screaming thus embarrassing himself.

"Very well, Mr. President, uh Don, I will be there."

"When you arrive, you had best change your fucking attitude and make sure you are clean and your breath doesn't smell like a distillery. I can almost smell it from here. Trump out."

"He doesn't play games, does he?" mentioned the senator putting away his drink.

"Can't afford to," mentioned Sam.

Several other "reminders" were made to other leaders and only a couple had to be brought in early that morning. The breakfast was good yet the information presented was the greatest shock to nearly everyone present.

"Alright, I signed some executive orders last night fulfilling my campaign promises or the ones I was able to do by law and in this manner. The first one is the ban on all political parties..."

"What the hell are you saying, uh Sir!" stood and shouted the former House majority leader.

"Sit down and shut up, congressman! I made a promise."

"You can't do this," the irate representative continued to shout but this time sitting down.

"Just did."

"Then who are the minority and majority leaders?"

"There is no minority and there is no majority. Your leadership does not depend upon your party affiliation or tenure but on your quality and work ethics. You will elect one leader which is more of a spokesperson and will have twenty-four hours to get it done. If not, I will select one from the House and the vice president will do the same from the Senate. Just get it done either your way or mine. Eat your breakfast. You can also talk with the former president or vice president if you have any issues or set up an appointment with me. Each of you has my schedule but don't come bitching and complaining. We have a country to run. I fucked it up enough when I was president and it's taken another administration to try and repair the damage I made."

Other executive orders he had signed during the night included his promises of a flat sales tax which meant removing any federal income tax. It was fair and had been highly supported by not only his supporters but also those of the other candidates who embraced the idea and policy. With a reduced staff in the department of the Internal Revenue Service or IRS, none were without jobs as other agencies took them on with some opting for early retirement.

All marriage licenses now had expiration dates on them just as a business license would which meant if one did not renew said license which could be one, five or ten year documents, the marriage would be over or expired. Divorce attorneys still had jobs due to dealing with community property disputes.

Any prisoners sentenced to death would be immediately executed but had to have had at least two unsuccessful appeals. They were to have the option of taking their own lives with a fast-acting pill similar to those used by CIA agents in the event they were captured or any other form of their choice. Also, any prisoner sentenced to either long term incarcerations or life without parole could be given that same option.

A national lottery was established to help further balance the federal budget. Many displaced IRS workers would be assigned to these duties which would be part of the IRS.

Doctor-assisted suicide was now legal but only in cases where there was no hope of a cure and this was to be death with dignity and painless.

Young people were becoming more and more disrespectful and schools becoming more violent with the education levels falling drastically. America was basically a joke when it came to public education. Also, the infrastructure in the country was on a decline so the order was that any child who either dropped out of school before obtaining a high school diploma or was a constant disruption to the school including multiple brushes with law enforcement were to be inducted into the military for a term of no less than two years. After basic training, they were to be assigned various duties from construction to planting trees and upgrading schools and other facilities while at the same time learning discipline and some form of trade as well as earning their high school requirements. For every year of service also meant one year of free college, university or trade school education.

With these orders in place, effective immediately, change was being felt and also, the promises of Donald Trump were seen unlike the promises he had made and didn't keep in his first administration. The American people found this Trump to be a man of his word and one who never took a day off unless he had to travel to meet some world leader but that was actually work. He had lots of golf clubs but auctioned them off for charity and his only time he was not in the office was when he was in the gym pumping massive amounts of weight with his friend and second in command Robert Sims. Sometimes he walked the grounds of the White House with Baby, the first lady and Dolly but often only with himself and the large feline. It was not uncommon for him to speak with the grounds staff sometimes bringing them small meals and inviting them to have lunch with him. This was the president of dreams.

As the presidency continued toward the end of the second year of his term, the pandemic once again showed its ugly face. For the most part it had been under control yet another form appeared. This other strain was more virulent and nothing the world had ever known. People were literally dropping dead on the streets in every city of the globe. There were times when he would greet his secretary in the morning and upon leaving at the noon hour found her dead at her desk and often when a replacement came in an hour later did not survive the day. It was sad that one evening when he returned to the residence and began talking to his wife discovered she had died during the afternoon along with his young son. With people dropping dead at an alarming rate burials became illegal often to the point of mass cremations.

"Why am I not dead?" he asked his scientific advisors.

After taking numerous samples, it was determined that he was immune so he quickly volunteered to give as much of his blood to hopefully find a cure. Still, the population of every country continued to die. There were none of those zombie or psychotic-like mutations from the movies and it seemed only himself, Robert and Ho were the ones who had some resistance. It also had no effect on animals. World leaders were at a loss and by the end of his third year in office, there were hardly any people in America to have an election. Sometimes even during a cabinet meeting one member would suddenly die and he often wondered how many would survive the night. The scientists realized after over a year of making zero advances in finding any sort of vaccine, all that could happen was to let it run its course. He hated going to bed because when he awoke he wondered who would be left.

Part 4

Chapter I

When he awoke as usual well before dawn, something was different. The feel was different as was the smell and sounds. As his mind and senses adjusted, he began to realize he was no longer in his comfortable bed that he had once shared with his wife, the reinstated First Lady of the United States along with Baby the First Cat. He was back on Alcatraz. Which one had been the dream? Would he wake up the next day back in the White House or was this where he was to remain? It wasn't long before he came to the conclusion that this one at that moment he was in reality. He was on The Rock. It had been a good dream, a dream filled with knowledge, love, redemption but sadness as well. Since he had retained the skills in the previous life or dream from the first one, the one where he was now, he began to wonder if such would be the case in this reality. Only time would tell. He had been happy in his previous existence with his wife, the discipline, the cat and training but he had also been happy in the one before which was the one he had at the moment. He had been happy in the dream that is until the pandemic had ravaged the world, the pandemic which he realized in many ways was his fault. He hadn't created it but he had promoted it with the rallies and unsafe practices while ignoring the advice of those who knew more than he ever would or at least in the first presidency. In the second one, the virus had apparently been lying dormant and then re-emerged stronger than ever so he blamed himself. Then he began to wonder would they be sending more killers, more of the vermin of society for him to thin out or for them to end the proverbial wart on the ass of society meaning him, he could only take a wait and see attitude yet he had to prepare. If, however, the pandemic was raging, there might not be anyone to send. There were traps to set and to be vigilant plus he had to train, which was something he had learned to do on his own.

Arming himself with the knives and two bows, one for hunting and one for fishing, then a quick breakfast before he began to make the tour of the coastline where he had set numerous lethal traps. It was similar to setting out a series of trot lines for fishing hoping to get as many as possible. As luck would have it, he was successful as he had bagged the limit with five that day. It was a simple matter of removing the heads, placing them in his backpack, stripping the bodies of all clothing, packs and weapons before tossing them into the sea and allowing them to go out with the tide. Some of the sharks had actually gotten to know him and frequently followed him awaiting for an easy meal. Today they were not disappointed. Heads were then processed and skulls placed on poles for others to see. Sometimes when a smaller fish came within range, he took it out with the bow and he did spot one nice tuna cruising slowly which made it an easy meal. It was just a matter of using a special arrow with line attached and the shot was made, all within less than one minute. The fish was perhaps thirty pounds and was gutted and added to the heavy pack. Once butchered, most were put in the smoker for at least a week's worth of meals.

After the heads were put in a large kettle of boiling water that sat outside in what used to be the prison recreation area, the fish was processed before he headed to the library to read the news online. As usual it did point out that there was a new strain of the virus that everyone felt was under control but had begun to spread rapidly and was much faster in the way it killed. Some reports were of people dying in their beds or on buses as they went about their daily business.

"This is not good," he thought, "but I am here, safe to some degree that is unless they bring it along with the monthly deliveries."

Actually, Inmate 045 had gotten to the point where he was self-sufficient and kind of hoped they would no longer continue this operation. Little did he know that the ones in charge had already made that decision hoping they could starve him to death and end having to even think of the inconvenience of having to even care for him in some way. He should have been dead long before but for some reason continued to survive. They had sent more than three hundred types of killers to the island plus a few annoying reporters. All had been unsuccessful. Now with the pandemic starting back, there were other concerns than a single former president in exile on a large boulder in the middle of San Francisco Bay. He had declared it to be his own country, the Republic of Alcatraz with him the supreme leader.

As the heads were being processed in the boiling water removing all traces of who these individuals were cooking away the flesh, allowing the brains inside to become a gelatinous mass that easily poured from the eyes and ears, he decided to take another stroll around the grounds, stopping to check on the sheep and goats along with the progress of the garden, picking a vegetable or two for an easy and nutritious snack. He thought about the dream and the cat. It was odd that the very second that image entered his mind, he heard the cries of a small kitten overhead. There less than thirty yards to the west, he saw a hawk with what must have been a newborn cat in its talons crying in pain. Instinctively, the arrowed was notched, drawn and fired in one smooth motion striking the bird in the neck killing it instantly as it began to plummet toward a clump of small bushes nearby without releasing the animal, its hopeful meal. Fortunately, due to the feathers of the flying predator, it did not fall quickly which gave Don time to run toward it catching it before it hit the ground.

Upon inspection, the small perhaps two day old baby cougar or puma appeared not to be seriously injured yet was in distress, nonetheless. Don always carried supplies with him including containers for water or other items he felt might be of use so it was a simple matter of milking one of the nanny goats who had become very affectionate to him so taking some milk was not uncommon and she readily complied. As he put some of it on his fingers and placed it on the kitten's mouth, it immediately took it. When they reached the kitchen, at first an eye dropper was located which filled its belly and later a small rubber surgical glove would be filled with the liquid and a hole pricked in the end of one finger which would act as a nipple. As it fed, he carefully and painlessly applied some antibiotic cream to the wounds and covered them with gauze and bandages. They didn't appear to be very deep and there was little bleeding which made him realize that the little one should more than likely survive. Like the dream, he now had a cat, a puma, a friend which he naturally called Baby. It couldn't have been more than a couple of days old with its eyes still closed like the one in the dream. At least he remembered how to care for it but it would have been nice to have had a mother cat to do the work but he would have to act in that role.

With having had a set routine in this world, this reality, a diversion such as the kitten was welcomed and Don took to it with the discipline he had developed in both worlds. Now, during every waking moment and often caring for the young

ALCATRAZ AWAITS: THE LEGACY OF DONALD TRUMP

female during the night, he devoted his time to the kitten or more precisely and accurately the cub. Like in the other animal, Baby needed care especially since it had been wounded. The bird, a type of hawk was prepared for a meal and some of its softer feathers combined with the wool of the sheep and goats to make a nice comfortable bedding. Inmate 045 had gotten skilled at providing for himself and had hundreds of rabbit pelts stacked in various places, some sewn into huge blankets and rugs. Meat had been smoked and dried and he had more than he could eat in years. Now he had more reasons to catch fish and harvest some fresh meat. He knew that within a few months, the young feline would be trying to develop skills in hunting on her own.

The rabbits had pretty much over populated the island and many times, Don found himself killing them to be used as bait for catching some of the larger sharks. He had fashioned some massive hooks which he attached to a combination of chains and heavy ropes. Then he took some of the plastic that various foods were shipped in to use as floats and these were set adrift. The largest shark he had caught was well over fourteen feet in length but the average around six or eight. Sharks have many uses from the nutritional oil in their livers to their skin and teeth and after living on the island for more than three years, he learned many skills plus with the people he killed acquired a vast assortment of implements to sustain himself. He even prepared for the possibility that the water maker might shut down so rain water was collected and he was very conservative with its usage. Many large cisterns were filled to capacity and kept at high levels at all times. Yes, he had everything he needed to live on but his companions were limited to the sheep and goats. Now he had Baby. If the pandemic continued to ravage the world, he knew he would have to find some way of making it to the mainland but when the opportunity arose, he would take advantage of it.

Chapter 2

Within two weeks, Baby's eyes had opened and she immediately bonded with the first one she saw and that was Don or Inmate 045. From that moment on, the cub was his constant companion as he introduced it to the sheep and goats which took to it like the human. With this bonding, the feline realized these were his friends, not his food. The rabbits on the other hand were different as were the rats and within a month after Baby had opened her eyes, she began hunting them often piling them up in a special place to be proudly displayed just as her "daddy" had with the skulls of the invaders which by the way were becoming fewer, eventually quit coming but never once did he let his guard down.

While Baby was developing, he began to recall the previous reality or dream and remembered what the man named Ho had taught him about accessing information and how he had learned many languages including those spoken by animals. At first he tested it on the sheep and goats where they discovered they understood him and he in turn returned the favor. With this success, he tried it on the cub who immediately knew what was going on. Apparently animals are born without having to learn their language or at least the fundamentals of it so when her eyes opened, she could immediately speak with Don as she would with any other member of her species. This way he could teach her how to hunt and what to kill and what not to.

In the nation's capital, as the pandemic continued to decimate the population, Sam and Jack continued to monitor the situation on the island but with less enthusiasm. Whether End Mate was still in operation didn't matter yet they were finally told that there would be one more attempt on the former president's life and that would be the end of it. Basically, they were running out of candidates and were more concerned about survival than something like Donald J. Trump.

"So what's he up to now, Sam? My wife died yesterday, you know."

"Sorry to hear that. Mother died this morning."

"How much longer for us do you think?"

"Hard to say but Inmate 045 seems to be doing well. He's got a cat you know."

"Cat? How?"

"Got me but must have been a few months ago. Thought I told you. Looks like a puma."

"Damn! Big fucker isn't it? Alright I just got word that Operation End Mate will be shutting down. They are running out of inmates. They are sending twenty more and that will be the end of it and hopefully the end of Trump. They quit sending supplies months ago but he's doing fine."

"When's the final assault?"

"First thing in the morning and then you and I have been ordered to go home. D. C's a ghost town anyway so if we survive we survive. Fuck Trump."

On The Rock, Inmate 045 never let his guard down and was happy he had remained vigilant. As the early morning fog lifted, he saw the approach of a large vessel, larger than usual with what he estimated to be at least twenty passengers of various descriptions. The seas that day were rough due to the heavy and sustained winds which gave him and Baby time to greet them. The ones on the vessel had no idea what to expect or were only told it was the former president who they only knew was lazy and overweight which was enough for them. Don informed the cat what he wanted her to do and that was hop on the canvas roof of the boat quietly when they arrived and then begin growling as loud as she could for about ten seconds before leaping into the middle of the group biting and clawing them before getting out quickly.

"After you are free of them, I will begin shooting them and we will go together and you will bite them in the throats and I will do rest."

As instructed, as soon as the boat began to dock at the pier, the large cat silently jumped onto the grey canvas roof and began growling like a real lion.

"Fuck! There's a lion!" one shouted in fear.

"Where?" asked another looking in all directions.

Then all hell broke loose as the cat was in the middle of them clawing and biting everything in sight before making a mad dash onto the pier and up the hill where Don awaited with his bow in which within a matter of seconds ten of the invaders were either dead or dying while the men in suits watched from what they assumed was the safety of the other vessel. Then the two of them, man and animal casually walked down the hill.

"You're Donald Trump," one asked.

"King Donald the First to you, corpse."

"King?"

With no other words spoken except in Puma, the man and the cat began to kill the remaining assassins. Then spotting the men on the other boat, they were killed in rapid succession with deadly razor sharp arrows as they tried to get away with the engines at full throttle. The course had not been set it heading out to open waters soon out of sight. With twenty bodies to dispose of they took a while to process but by the end of the day were all part of the trophy collection and many in the bellies of the creatures who cruised along the shore.

"You did a great job, Baby," he said as he stroked her behind her ears with love and in her language.

There was a bond between the cat and the man. They were best friends. They were family. He had told her that there might be others like those they had met and killed that morning and they had to always be on guard. Little did he know that the group that had been killed was the last and the operation was over. The pandemic was sweeping the nation and the world but he was safe on his island. No deliveries of any form had been sent in months but he knew that at some point he had to find a way of leaving his place and at least seeing how much of mankind remained but for now he would monitor the seas and internet to gather information.

Don knew that he was the one who was responsible for the pandemic's spread for the most part in this reality or at least blamed himself and there was not a day that went by when he didn't regret his actions or inactions but that was a different time and a different man or someone who claimed to be one and there was nothing he could do except accept his fate. He didn't think he was a bad person now and actually didn't think he was bad or good; he simply existed. Baby loved him as did the sheep and goats. His health was good in fact better than it had ever been in his entire life. Now he had to plot his escape from his island, his republic, his country.

Chapter 3

More than a year went by when fate brought him the opportunity he desired. There she was, a ship, a sailing vessel, a catamaran to be exact drifting with the current perhaps some one hundred yards or a bit more off the north-west coast of Alcatraz. He had considered the vessel that the would-be assassins had arrived in but after viewing it, discovered it was quite antiquated and would not have survived for very long on the open seas. Basically, it was what is or was known as a rust bucket. As he had learned in the previous reality or dream or whatever you wished to call it, how to harness energy he had begun spending many long hours developing the powers of moving objects with his mind. He had also taught this to Baby and it got to where they could capture or kill rabbits with ease. Therefore, as he stood with the large cat beside him, he told her in her language to focus on bringing the ship near the shore. Within moments it began to move at first slowly and then with greater speed until it was within ten yards of them. The area was rocky so they directed it to the pier where it was gently docked and secured.

As they cautiously boarded the vessel knife in hand while the cat sniffed the air, her ears back they discovered no life of any sorts and no bodies anywhere. There were notes in the log about destinations and such and apparently the ship, a large one of twenty meters appeared to have been owned by a family from Vancouver, Canada. Pictures were on display of a husband, wife and two teenage twin sons. There was nothing indicating the fate of the owners except that they had encountered a storm but that was more than six months earlier with no other recent entries.

As they searched the ship, Don found several hidden compartments and realized this was not a simple innocent family but gun runners. Perhaps the photos were fake as a distraction but the guns were real. There were literally hundreds of them plus enough ammunition, magazines, knives, grenades and body armor to supply a small army. Other compartments were found, some containing drugs which were gathered to either be tossed over the side or buried yet depending on the population might be saved and used as barter since he had no money. It was odd that the very second the thought of money came to mind, he spotted another compartment and upon opening discovered stacks upon stacks of cash of many types such as pounds, Chinese yuan but mostly United States dollars along with over a dozen wooden boxes containing tens of thousands of gold coins. There were also stacks of bars he recognized easily as gold, silver, copper, steel and titanium. Instantly, knowledge of how to forge various weapons from many of these came to him. Later, he realized he would construct a forge and even though he had a large assortment of knives, he felt a need for several swords of Japanese design as well as new arrows along with the more lethal broad heads.

The ship itself was apparently brand new. Obviously not cheap by any standards with elegant wood finish, marble, granite and glass table tops, a state of the art water maker and various forms of power making it or her self-sufficient. She was white to the waterline and navy blue below on its twin hulls yet upon further inspection found a third sub-hull between the two main ones in which he discovered was nearly completely one piece of a form of synthetic glass or polymer which allowed him to view the life below the surface and even control the vessel. There were two large masts with snow white sails and for the most part nearly everything was automated. Since he had no idea as to how to pilot a sailing ship, this would come in handy making it easier to navigate. A small lifeboat or zodiac was secured and towed behind which he also found housed survival gear, water purifier, weapons, fishing equipment and the like. Inside the ship there was every form of convenience possible from large bathroom and shower to laundry room and two bedrooms simple yet comfortable each having retractable curtains on the near wraparound windows and large skylights making it easy to watch the stars. Kitchen housed one large refrigerator along with a separate freezer, food dehydrator and vacuum sealer. There was also an indoor grill and hot air cooker. Upon further investigation he found a storage area where more than half a dozen fishing rods and reels were housed plus nets of various types including drift, landing and cast nets.

As he began to complete scanning every inch of the ship, he looked around and found his feline companion slumbering on a plush sheepskin rug in front of a large tv screen.

"Well, at least we know you like it, Baby," he thought with a smile.

It was also odd that there was a sizable office with two computers, the data which he would view later on but he did notice several files loaded with movies that he felt would be a great way to pass the time. Another thing that caught his attention was the refrigerator, freezer and cabinets were nearly completely stocked with all of the necessary items plus some luxury ones including Belgium chocolate and very expensive tins of caviar and coffee. Apparently the former occupants had come from Asia as there were some frozen king crab legs. When he was looking through the fishing gear he had found a collapsible crab trap and a hoist with large spool of heavy cord apparently for catching these creatures in the Bering Sea.

"Now that I have a ship, all I have to do is learn how to sail," he puzzled while sporting a grin.

Within a couple of more minutes he began a more detailed search of the ship finally coming to one of the control centers one of three with the first above the main deck, the other just off the galley and the third in the sub-hull. As he looked at the controls themselves, they were surprisingly simple and in basic English. There was a menu with all commands laid out especially the one that said "destination."

"Okay, I want to go to Washington," he said under his breath but instead of punching in the location, he felt it best to make the necessary preparations beforehand.

The sails had come down and were stored in some metal horizontal tubes extending from the steel masts which made him realize just how automated the vessel was. Lots of things to consider such as acquiring money or at least things he could use as barter. There were becoming fewer and fewer new items online which meant the people who managed the sites were dying out. During one of the last reports was that the population of the United States was down to five percent of what it had been when he had been president. It was sad that he realized that he was the one who was responsible for the deaths of so many due to his selfishness and had to accept his fate. So many things to consider but he did have plenty of time.

"Baby," he called, "time to head to the house."

The cat was never annoyed to be awakened and responded with the kitten in her. They definitely had work to do such as harvesting as many rabbits as possible, sheering sheep to make more rugs, blankets and garments along with cheese. Lately he had caught several large salmon without hardly any effort so he had to set out the trot lines to catch more which would be smoked, dried and vacuum sealed in the hundreds of bags he had at his disposal. With the zodiac, he could extend his fishing area to greater depths and acquire larger fish plus with the guns, he could kill off a large number of seals and sea lions for their heavy protein-laden flesh and dense fur. For some reason he knew each firearm by its appearance and understood how to use them. This meant he simply picked up one of the larger caliber ones, loaded a magazine, found a perfect place and chose five of the larger adults of the group and made sure each shot counted. They were precise and painless to the brain stem, all in right at five seconds. There was a suppressor or silencer if you wish attached to the weapon muffling the sounds and the others hardly knew what was going on until the last one fell. It took nearly the entire day to skin and process the meat where it was placed for nearly two days in the smoker. Naturally, Baby reaped the benefits practically gorging herself and even gnawing on the bones.

    The forge was also made and within less than a month had created nearly a dozen elegant and effective swords which he tested on the beef and pork carcasses as well as a few medium-sized pine and cedar trees while discovering that due to the combination of materials especially the titanium, went through these like a hot blade through warm butter.

    Days, weeks and months passed before he realized it was time to leave. It was mid-spring and the weather was pleasant. Information online was becoming less and less. Reports of the population of the United States had it practically decimated down to pre-colonial times. The lights of the once vibrant and bustling city of San Francisco had become fewer over the past year and now he could only spot a few here and there which appeared to be camp fires. Also naval and air traffic had become practically nonexistent and during the last month had not seen a single craft of any sort except for the one he had named "Ghost" the catamaran which would be his means of escaping from his exile.

It took just shy of a week to load the ship and go over where he had lived for nearly four years, checking, double checking just to make sure before he made the decision to set sail. He had familiarized himself with every detail of running the ship and found her to be one of the most technologically advanced vessels he had imagined. It was as if it was designed to be captained by someone with no experience whatsoever. All he had to do was plot a course and the system did everything. Full navigation, raising, lowering and adjusting sails, radar and sonar and even fish finders. Naturally he brought in several large dumbbells in order to maintain his muscle mass. Inmate 045 did have some concerns that if he landed in what was once a large American city, whether he would be exposed to the virus and if he would become a victim himself so he felt it best to plot a course to the nation's capital and avoid land as much as possible. He did find one compartment that was probably his best treasure trove of all as it contained several bio-suits which oddly enough displayed the NASA logo. They were basically spacesuits and one of them fit him perfectly despite his massive size yet he discovered these to be self-adjusting. Perhaps he might wait until he reached some of the smaller islands off the Mexican coast to gather fresh supplies and stretch his legs and those of his companion. As he had studied the navigation of the ship, he found he could easily interrupt the course by simply pushing a button that said "diversion" which would allow him to go wherever he wished and then press "resume" at which the former destination would be the same.

One more final check and just before dawn they were gone, heading to open seas.

Chapter 4

Donald Trump who no longer considered himself as Inmate 045 was ready. It was an hour before dawn and for the first time in four years put on his watch but then hesitated and put on one of the many he had found in a drawer at the desk in the office. It was a simple one, a sports watch, black and seaworthy which he hoped would suit the situation. Wealth no longer concerned him and a piece of jewelry that incidentally told time seemed meaningless. He was wearing what he had been wearing for most of his incarceration, military garb yet he did expect soon to shed some of it especially the boots. Naturally, he was armed with the, what he called the Rambo knife on his right hip and two Italian-made stainless steel handguns under each armpit both loaded and ready for action. Baby was also ready and she knew something wonderful was about to happen.

Sitting at the controls, the one located just off the galley, it was a now or never situation.

"Okay, here goes nothing," he said as he typed in Washington, D. C. where it said destination and then pressed the enter command.

Within seconds, a flurry of activity began. A small engine started and the ship began to move, first slowly and then gradually attaining speed reaching what had once been the shipping lanes before a moment of silence. Don's heart stopped or appeared to do so for what seemed to be an eternity along with his breath thinking that something must have gone wrong. Then everything started up once more. The sails slowly emerged from their secured tubes at the bases of the masts silhouettes against the light of the full orange moon at his shoulder gradually unfurling filling with wind until at full billow. On the screen it indicated the GPS coordinates, current location and a red dotted line to the nation's capital along with the estimated time of arrival at current speed.

"Three months, two days, eleven hours to Washington," he said out loud. Then he realized he had to make sure he had added the DC abbreviation to it because that's all he needed was to be like Columbus heading one way to get to another.

"Looks like we have some time, eh Baby," he continued.

With the ship underway he mentioned the word "breakfast" at which the large feline immediately responded. It was a simple matter of taking some of the fresh salmon he had caught the day before, cutting a large chunk and handing it to his companion, patting her head while he fired up the grill for the rest. It didn't take long before they were both sitting at the table or him at the table and Baby at his feet enjoying their first meal of the voyage.

Meal completed and everything nice and orderly, cleaned and as it was, he felt it would be a good idea to try his hand at fishing on the soon to be open seas. Heading south, the island of Alcatraz was growing smaller as he glanced over his left shoulder and then turned with reverence saluting and sending his respectful farewells to his former home, his former place of exile. In some ways he felt like Napoleon as he was escaping from Elba with the exception that the emperor had loyal subjects awaiting and supporting him whereas Don was unsure of who if any of his former loyalties or minions were even alive. Only time would tell and he seemed to have the clock and calendar on his side or so he hoped. For now, all he could do was allow time to pass and enjoy the moment.

Going out on deck, he made a few casts with light tackle and much to his surprise landed several foot long Spanish mackerel the first of which he gave to the already full cat who took her time munching on them. Two more were placed in the rotisserie where they were broiled to be eaten later on. For fun, he tried his hand with the cast net. It took several tries but soon he got the hang of it eventually creating a full ten foot diameter circular cast which after several tries allowed him a bounty of nearly one hundred shrimp and half a dozen cuttlefish plus a few fish he could not easily identify which he kept with the thoughts that he might troll them behind the ship on some of the heavier rigs with the hope of fighting perhaps a marlin or large tuna as he had seen on various shows in his younger days. The ship was moving steadily neither fast nor slow and with is full automation there was little if anything he could do. This gave him time to perform other duties such as clean the spacious home on the sea plus use a brush on the coat of his adoring companion. The cat knew not to try and sharpen her claws on any item within the ship but Don had brought along a piece of wood wrapped in a double layer of natural rope which he stood in one corner which she frequented at times. It was nice having movies many of which he had seen but some that were completely new to him. With the new system, he also realized that now he could communicate with others and was tempted to do so yet then hesitated because if he did try to contact people, he might be either blown out of the water or at the very least returned to the island. Instead, he checked his emails wading through tens of thousands of them viewing while not responding to any.

Despite being exiled and looked upon as a president who had been convicted of numerous crimes against his own country and the people of which he was to have served he had to be cautious

Alcatraz Awaits: The Legacy of Donald Trump

because he was now at that very moment an escaped convict. History was judging him harshly yet when he thought of it, he realized it probably wasn't harsh enough. The world was dead for the most part because of him and his self-centered attitude with near zero empathy. He had argued with people about things he had known little or nothing about always wanting the spotlight while convincing his many lower educated followers that he was an expert on virtually everything including medicine. When he thought of those days and that person, it did bring tears to his eyes and for nearly an hour he sobbed like a child. There was nothing he could do about past transgressions yet did hope and pray that he would live long enough to rectify them in some way.

The days passed well and for the most part the weather was cooperative. Fishing was plentiful and only a few times did he decide to open some of the packages of dried or frozen meat. There was plenty of rabbit but he had stripped the flesh of the remaining beef, mutton and pork carcasses, even processing their bones which he found to be excellent additions to soups yet also made some into weapons which he hoped he would never have to use. After more than a week, he spotted a small island to the west and felt it to be a good idea to explore the place so he entered the word "diversion" in the navigation system and then took command, steering the vessel to a small bay where he anchored. It was just after dusk and he spotted no lights or fires yet he did ask the computer about any human inhabitants at which nearly instantly gave the name of the island and notified him that there were no human life forms. In the morning he would take the zodiac along with two handguns, his bow, knives, vest with extra magazines as well as a quiver and adequate supply of arrows all equipped with the lethal heads. Before dawn after a good sleep, he and Baby were ready but instead of going directly to shore, felt it best to cruise around the place doubting the word of the computer. Who knows, maybe others had landed the night before so he had to be careful.

The bay was nice where the ship, the "Ghost" was secured with grass flats where there would typically be an abundance of scallops, oyster beds and others plus a nice drop off where he was certain to find large fish and perhaps stone crabs and lobsters. On a second thought before taking the smaller craft, he set out the crab trap in which he baited with heads and other remains from some of the fish he had caught earlier the day before. Only at that moment did he feel he was ready.

After checking to see if there were any people on the island from the safety of about twenty yards from the shore, only then did he decide to beach the small craft in sight of the larger one anchored in the bay. The cat knew to be on full alert and the man had his bow ready even though he could have brought any of the numerous military weapons he had at his disposal but he was comfortable with the more primitive instrument. He noticed there had been some paths but attributed them to the possibility of animals such wild pigs by watching Baby, he knew that there must be some in the area but none nearby.

For nearly twenty minutes avoiding dense undergrowth, he came across an encampment or some sort. There were houses mostly made of wood and stone with thatched roofs many in need of repair plus a stream with a dilapidated paddle wheel and off to the side was what appeared to be a church cemetery yet none of the graves were fresh. Entering the holy structure, while remaining even more vigilant, he spotted a figure. It was dressed in black with its back to him and a white collar around its neck indicating it was indeed a priest.

"Excuse me Father but I thought this place was devoid of human life. Uh, Father?" he continued to speak but louder each time.

Then once more before, he touched the back of the form at which it fell to the floor in a crumpled mass of bones! Apparently, the man had been dead for years and was the only survivor. Then something odd caught Don's eye. It was a calendar.

"This can't be right," he said. "The date says twenty years from the time I thought I had left Alcatraz."

At that moment, Don realized he had lost complete track of time. What he had thought had only been four years had actually been twenty. Apparently, the times on the computers had slowed down and even he must have slowed down. Perhaps the dreams had not been only for one night but for several years but nothing on the island seemed to have aged. He then began to theorize that the messages and sites on the internet were from the past and not the present. Now he had to find out if civilization existed at all.

There was no need in burying the priest but he did gather up some books and other items he felt might be useful. Then just as he was leaving the structure, Baby began to growl, her ears back and hair standing up on her back crouching low.

Before he could ask the cat what was going on, a large group of wild pigs, boars with six inch tusks emerged from the forest. Sensing the man and predator companion, began to charge but were no match for either. Don killed the first two easily with the simultaneous shots to the throats killing them instantly as Baby instinctively went for the throat of one of the larger ones which gave the man time to remove the handguns and began firing on the remaining four. Six others opted to retreat to the safety of the jungle. Then silence. There it was not even mid-morning and it had been a long day already. Okay, so time on Alcatraz had nearly stopped. He got that, well sort of. Okay, apparently he had not aged. He got that too, in a way. Now he was on a small island apparently part of Mexico in which an entire village was dead and he began to wonder if what he saw here was any indication of what was to be seen with the rest of the world. Why hadn't the food in the catamaran aged? This was sounding like something out of a science fiction movie or mind of someone who would write such things.

"The hell with this shit," he said. "We have boars to skin and meat to process. Right, Baby?"

The cat seemed to agree and soon he was busy butchering the seven large animals and by the middle of the afternoon had completed the daunting task. It was hard work but worth it. With so much meat, he felt it best to go ahead and cook the animals in a large pit. A simple matter he had seen the people of Hawaii perform and also like the clam bakes in Maine where clams and lobsters were placed in moist seaweed over hot embers and covered for several hours. Therefore in less than an hour after the pit had been dug, the fire was blazing and an hour later, the meat was encased in the seaweed and the cooking began. Now it was just a matter of waiting and hoping the other pigs did not return although in some ways he secretly hoped they would.

Entering some of the houses, he continued to see calendars with the same year which further confirmed everything. There were a few items he felt he could use and also felt he might stay for a while. He did go to the beach where he found a nice selection of various shellfish such as scallops and oysters and then headed to the ship to check on the trap where as luck would have it was nearly loaded with lobsters, stone crabs and even an octopus which he released. The trap was reset with the hope that more would attempt to take the bait during the night.

"I'll get you later," he said as he tossed the slimy creature back into the sea.

He had checked on any shipping or air traffic in the area and there was none so he returned to the village where fires were set and the shellfish added to the pit which were ready within an hour or just in time for his dinner. Some of the meat had been kept out and placed on sticks over a smouldering fire for him and Baby as some of the raw flesh given to his furry friend. Fires were set in various areas around the village or where he was planning on spending the night mostly to guard the cooking meat from any animal that wished to take any but before nightfall, he had found an abundant supply of fruits of all sorts some of which he ate while some he would take later on.

Chapter 5

Don actually enjoyed a good sleep and with the puma by his side, he was able to rely on her keen senses to alert him if there was any breach of security. In the morning the meat was processed and hides continued to tan. It would take a few days but one thing he seemed to have was time and given such, allowed him to explore the island while mostly harvesting coconuts, bananas, shellfish and other commodities. With the powers of telekinesis there were times when he only had to point or direct his thoughts to a certain object and will it to come to him. Sometimes Baby got into the act literally reeling in a helpless mouse or other animal which she devoured with ease. He did kill nearly a dozen large non-venomous snakes and arboreal lizards which were skinned and the meat added to the menu so after a little less than a week he was pushed the *resume course* button and the ship continued onward. It was odd though that now the ship's computers were saying the current date which had been the same when he was on Alcatraz but now had apparently reset which meant he had lost right at twenty years. Don felt fine. In fact, he felt younger than he had felt in years but attributed this to his training and simple yet healthy lifestyle along with the meditations which brought him a sense of peace. Before he left the small island, he did bury the remains of the priest giving him the respect he wish he had.

Alcatraz Awaits: The Legacy of Donald Trump

After a little more than a month, taking his time and doing some island hopping along the way, it was announced that there was to be a course change as the isthmus of Panama was approaching. He wondered if with the decimated population whether he would be able to make it through since the locks had to be manned. When he got to the first lock, he found there was no lock at all as it has been completely destroyed so he continued onward. Since he had left Alcatraz, the only signs he had seen of human life were their remains. There were numerous ships littering the area some in his path while others were simply wrecks on the shoreline as nature began to engulf them. It was also interesting that he had neither seen nor heard of any primates whatsoever so apparently the virus had mutated enough not only to attack humans but those related to them. There were many graves and the obvious lone skeletal remains of the survivor responsible for digging the last ones but enough time had passed for perfect decomposition. With this discovery, he theorized that the virus had run its course and he hoped it had completely vanished. If that was the case, though, it meant only one of two things with the first that he was the only human inhabitant of the entire planet or the second meaning there might be some who were immune and had established colonies that he had yet to find. Continuing to travel through the canal or what was left of it, he still saw no signs of human life.

Before getting to the other locks, he often anchored for a day or so to catch some of the varieties of fish either with the nets, traps or rods and reels. It was surprising to see the types of life he was able to find. Naturally there were those flesh eating piranha which he found to be very tasty and then for fun he set out small fish on heavier gear and spent literally hours fighting and bringing in some larger catfish, stingrays and other bottom feeders which he released. Whenever he began to run low on fruit, he and Baby

John H. Cary

took the smaller craft to the shore for a quick excursion before heading back to the safety of the *Ghost* or brought them to the ship using his powers. Often he would find villages or small cities in which skeletons were scattered in the streets, sidewalks and stores, all perfectly bleached which were indicators that they had been exposed to the elements for years. It was kind of sad seeing schools where he could see where children and teachers had died at their desks, the cafeteria, library or playground. With the lack or absence of human life, even the animals had retreated into the forest. He did come across some packs of dogs that tried to attack him yet were held at bay by the large cat at his side who ended up killing several while the handguns took out others.

With no more locks remaining, it was a simple matter of entering the waters of the Caribbean, a place that had been well known for its clear seas and abundant life. Don had only been there once and that was to check on some of his properties but had never really experienced the culture mainly because he was more focused on business and how he could make more money by mostly exploiting the locals in regard to paying low salaries while always thinking of as his book described with the "art of the deal." As the thoughts of the people he had hurt for the sake of making a profit, this saddened him and continued to realize that maybe this was his punishment for all the bad things he had done. He had not only been an awful president but mostly an awful person. Now was not the time to reflect on the past but to focus on what was ahead of him and of the present.

Compared to the Pacific, the Caribbean was no comparison. It was calm yet he knew that soon he would be entering what was called "hurricane season" that tended to spawn some of the most catastrophic natural disasters ever conceived. He remembered many of them with names such as Hugo and Katrina and even joked with the thought of one named after him.

Alcatraz Awaits: The Legacy of Donald Trump

"Yeah, Hurricane Donald. A lot of wind that causes a lot of damage," he began to laugh.

There were so many islands in the Caribbean and even though his destination was the nation's capital if the nation existed, he did enjoy this adventure in his life. After a couple of months on the sea, it became apparent that either his existence was no longer being noticed or that there was no one around to check on him. Still he had to find out if there were any survivors. Perhaps a few leaders existed in the seat of power but still he felt he could take his time. The GPS on the computer and navigation display indicated exactly where he was and the names of the former nations or perhaps current ones so he decided to spend a non-specific time exploring these places. In one of the compartments among the guns and ammunition, he found several masks, snorkels and swim fins so as he approached what was once the Cayman Islands, he diverted the ship from her intended destination, set the anchor in a bay of sorts, protected from any heavy seas that might occur, put on his gear which included his knife and took to the water. He informed the cat that he was going to find some food and not to worry. When he was on the island, his island of exile he had made one pair of shorts from the military fatigues which were excellent for his runs and now doubled as swimming trunks. They were comfortable and also had pockets and gave him a more military look. It was rather odd when he reflected back on his previous existence which he called his past life, that he often insulted the military even to the point of telling a telling one particular senator who had spent years in a prison in Vietnam that he didn't think he was a hero because he had been captured.

"Damn! I did say some stupid things," he said. "It's a wonder I had any friends at all or maybe they weren't really friends and only put up with me due to my money."

John H. Cary

Entering the water, he noticed that the aquatic life was quite abundant apparently due to the fact that there had been few if any humans in the area. He had a mesh bag with him tied to his right ankle and was also wearing gloves as another precaution. With the ship being a catamaran, it was able to handle shallower depths than most sailing vessels despite the addition of the sub-hull which allowed him to anchor at a depth of right at eight feet. It was a vast expanse of shallow water before tapering to more than twenty and beyond that at the mouth of the bay went on to more than several hundred. Don had experienced these places during the island hopping where he found what he was looking for primarily with the types of mollusks and crustaceans he was seeking for this upcoming meal and the meals to come. Even Baby had developed a taste for shellfish as she seemed more human than feline primarily since she had been raised by one. As luck would have it, he literally hit the jackpot easily taking six large spiny lobsters, three dozen scallops and an equal number of oysters.

As he was about to head to the catamaran, something caught his eye. It was a ship. A small one which appeared to be yacht with two masts that appeared to have hit something producing a gaping hole on the starboard side about mid-ship. It was nothing the likes of the *Ghost* but seemed large enough for four or six people at the very most. Since he was in top shape, he had discovered earlier that he could hold his breath almost infinitely and entered the vessel made a quick look to determine the passengers even though most of the pictures were waterlogged yet there was one that was sealed at which he found a photo of a father, mother and young girl who couldn't have been more than two or three. This made him wonder if anyone had survived and was on the island. It was not even mid-morning so he had plenty of time to explore along with his trusty sidekick.

Coming back onboard, he rinsed off quickly, made a quick meal of some of the catch and then armed himself and then he and the cat were in the zodiac heading toward the shore. Baby knew or sensed something was up and was told in her language what to expect.

"There might be humans on this island," he told her as they were boarding the small craft.

Not only was Don armed with his bow, quiver loaded with arrows but also with one Italian handgun as well as a heavier caliber American model under each armpit plus a knife on each hip, back pack with food, water and medical supplies. As another precaution, he slung one of the Japanese style swords over his shoulder. He had changed into the standard fatigues and boots along with a vest that housed five extra magazines for each weapon. The island itself wasn't that large, perhaps two miles long and a mile or so at the widest point with a mountain of sorts in the center. Aside from that, there was mostly dense jungle growth.

As he landed on the beach some twenty yards from the ship, the first thing he noticed were tracks. Some were animal of what appeared to be those annoying yet delicious wild pigs and then human footprints. Compared to his, they were small like that of a child and were recent so he knew that there was at least one survivor of the sunken ship. Still, he had to be cautious. It was a major convenience to have the large cat with him since her senses were indeed multiple times his yet she had been trained not to attack indiscriminately and if there was a child, she would be protected.

After more than twenty minutes mostly walking along the shoreline a well-traveled footpath was discovered. Essentially he had followed the tracks in reverse hoping to find their origin. Soon, he did find signs of human habitation. There was a small shelter within the canopy of trees about ten feet off the ground.

Immediately, Baby's ears went back and she crouched knowing something or someone was near.

"I'm Don and I'm not going to hurt you," he called.

"Promise?" came the meek reply.

"Cross my heart," he said kindly.

"Is that a lion?" asked what sounded like a young girl.

"Well, sort of but she's very friendly. Her name is Baby. Would you like to pet her? What's your name?"

"My name is Annie. You said you are Don and the lion's name is Baby?"

"Right."

"Okay Don. I will come out but I am afraid."

"It's alright. I would be afraid too. Are there any others here?"

"No. My parents died I forgot exactly when but it's just me."

A child appeared from behind a large tree. She was naked and dirty and couldn't have been more than six. Tanned skin, long blonde hair, blue eyes and round face.

"Baby, be good. This is our friend."

At that moment the cat began to approach the child purring like a large house cat even acting playful which brought a smile to the once frightened face. Then when she reached the girl, she began nuzzling the child rubbing her cheeks on her legs and buttocks wishing to be petted. Then she laid down acting as if she wanted her belly to be rubbed which made the girl start laughing.

"You can touch her and rub her belly if you like," came the warm reply from the former president and former inmate.

Soon the girl had no choice but to abide by the begging of the large cat who seemed to smile at her continuing to purr loudly just like any normal run of the mill cat would have done. Don approached slowly and the girl became more relaxed.'

"You have a lot of guns and knives. Is it because of the pigs?" she asked.

"Pigs? Oh yes, pigs. I saw their tracks on the beach. Are they a problem?"

"I am afraid of them but my mother and father made the house in the tree so they couldn't hurt us."

"What happened to your parents?" Don asked while sitting down opposite the child also stoking the large cat.

"They got sick a few years ago and blood came from their mouths and noses and one day my mother died so my father and I buried her over there," she pointed, "and then the next day he died so I had to bury him next to her."

At that she began to cry so Don reached out to comfort her as she accepted his embrace.

"It's alright Annie. We will take care of you. Are you hungry?" he asked reaching into his backpack.

"Oh, yes! I am very hungry but I know how to catch fish and eat bananas and other things. My parents taught me."

Don had brought along some smoked salmon and other items he had prepared which she ate like it was her first meal. As they sat with the cat, she explained when she was about three she and her parents were on the ship and had been on the sea for maybe a year or her earliest memories but then there was big storm at night and when they woke up, they were there and the ship was sinking. That's all she remembered. A year later her parents died and since then she has been all alone. Then early that morning she saw the *Ghost* and didn't understand what it was at first but was soon running from the pigs she heard coming.

"Okay Annie, you can come with Baby and I and we will look after you. Also, we need your help to run the ship, okay?"

"Yes, I would like that. I don't know how to read very well. Can you teach me?" she asked.

"Of course. I have lots of books. Go ahead and get your things and we will go."

"I don't have any things," she mentioned still munching on the food.

"No clothes? Nothing?"

"Do I need clothes?" she asked.

"I guess not at least for now but where we are going you might later. Okay, we won't worry about that. Let's head on to the beach and set sail."

As they were nearing the beach, Baby began to growl.

"I think Baby knows we are about to have company," Don mentioned in a whisper.

"Pigs! We have to run!" the girl shouted.

"It's okay, Annie. Here scurry up that tree and we will kill them. You will be safe."

"What about you?"

"We will be fine. We have met these guys before. Just watch and it will be over soon."

After helping the girl to a branch about six feet above the ground, he began unsheathing the sword. Don stood his ground and soon several large animals with thick sharp protruding tusks came at him and his companion. Baby took the first one nearly ripping its throat out and then Don parried decapitating one and while burying the blade nearly up to the hilt in the third. Loading the bow, an arrow entered the gaping mouth of another while one of the knives was thrown penetrating the skull of the fifth that was the end of it. There were two others but they opted to reverse course and were never seen again.

"That was fun," Don casually mentioned. "Annie, that's how we kill pigs. Now we have to skin them and get them ready for our dinners later on."

"Wow! You and Baby are good pig killers. We can eat these?" she asked while being helped from the tree.

"Yes, very delicious."

"Don, can you teach me how to use that thing you have, that uh…"

"The sword," he pointed holding it in his hand.

"Yes, sword. I would like to learn and how you shoot the other thing," she mentioned touching the bow.

"I can teach you anything you want. Just ask."

The girl was curious about everything so they went around looking for pieces of straight wood that could fit her hands even though he did have a couple of short Japanese style weapons that he knew would suffice but for now they might be a bit too dangerous. In the meantime, the pigs were butchered, skinned and prepared and were soon being cooked over several fires. While they were roasting, Don took the little girl to the ship to where she was introduced to the shower, soap and shampoo as well as the various parts of the floating home. She was dirty and in need of the basic necessities of civilization and insisted that he helped wash her back. Even though he offered her one of his green military shirts, she didn't see the need so he left it like that. Apparently, she had outgrown her clothes years ago and had gotten used to not wearing anything eventually viewing it as natural. She was a child, a little girl who needed to be cared for but Don did admire her since she was able to survive for over a year alone and apparently was immune to the virus.

Then pigs were processed and Annie loved how delicious they were. At first she ate like a savage using both hands shoving food into her mouth but soon began to copy the man. After a couple of days, they decided to set sail. The girl had bonded with Baby who had taken to her always rubbing against her and playing yet at the same time was very protective. Gradually, she also began to wear the large military t shirt to bed which gave her an extra feeling of security. There was an incident when Don was preparing the zodiac and a large boar came from the forest who began running toward the child who had been playing with the large feline near the edge of the forest. Immediately, the cat attacked it ripping large gashes on its hind legs, shoulders and throat. She didn't kill it but let the animal know who was the boss as it limped away in defeat. They had started their training with the wooden replicas of the sword and within a short time, the girl became rather adept in its usage. Don even allowed her to strike him a few times even though she felt bad when she did so instead he found a study tree in which she could practice making contact. On the ship with the extra bedroom Annie had her own place yet during the first night felt the need to sleep with the man who found it comforting to be able to hold a real person for the first time in ages. After that, she was content to stay in her own room often sharing the bed with the large cat who divided her time between the two humans.

For the next several weeks they spent sailing from point to point sometimes stopping to gather fruit and other items. Beaches were ideal places to train with the various weapons such as the bow and the child appeared to be a natural with this weapon as after only a couple of hours of instruction could hit a fist-sized target from up to thirty yards and was getting to the point of occasionally making hits on moving ones. For her protection she had to wear something such as shirt which she gradually grew accustomed to even though most of the time she wore nothing.

There were times when a wrecked ship was spotted only to find it either abandoned or littered with human remains in the form of skeletons bleached by the elements. In one such case the ship was quite large, apparently a cruise ship locked on a reef gradually being absorbed by nature so Don went onboard alone leaving the girl and cat on the catamaran simply to keep the child from seeing the carnage. As he explored, he found the cabins in which children had stayed which meant children's clothing. Before boarding, he had taken Annie's measurements and upon return after the first trip, had her the main things she needed and those were shoes. It had gotten to where her nudity wasn't even noticed but he knew that when they reached the cooler latitudes, she would have to wear something simply as protection against the cold. She had been going without garments for virtually her entire short life that she knew of no other way but as time wore on she realized she had to wear something when they were exploring just in case other people were discovered. On the ship and when they had the places to themselves after thoroughly scouting them, she preferred to be naked. The first load had clothes, food, a few tools and books whereas the second and third were mostly flash drives, extra laptops and what he thought the child would enjoy most and those were toys. He also picked up sports equipment mainly badminton items which they would use on the beaches where they would certainly stop.

Don enjoyed having the child around and eventually he began to see her as his own child and she began to call him Father as her memories of her parents began to fade. He began to theorize that perhaps he too was immune to the virus since obviously he had been exposed to it due to the numerous encounters with the remains of those who had fell victim to the pandemic.

About late summer, the winds began to gather with rough seas so he knew they had to find a safe harbor due to an impending storm. Without weather forecasters, all he could do was speculate. Looking at the map on the console, he found a place which used to be the island nation of Cuba. It had been a source of irritation to the United States yet had also begun to open its doors to the wealthy hence resorts and casinos. As they had been traveling, the girl had become his student learning to read and write among other things. She already knew the basics such as the English alphabet and was reading on a first or second grade level but this changed soon and within less than a month could read several years above her own. It got to the point to where she loved sitting on the plush rug with Baby as her pillow reading out loud to the large cat who seemed to be listening intently yet most of the time in deep sleep.

One time as they were heading to the next destination, upon awakening, she walked on the deck and saw Don and the cat meditating while performing the energy exercises levitating more than three feet of the surface as other objects hovered in mid-air. Instead of saying anything, she sat down in the same posture as the man, in silence and her eyes closed. Both were aware of the child and started helping her, guiding her silently providing her with some of the tools they had both acquired. Then after about another twenty minutes, the exercise was concluded at which time he explained what was going on.

"The world is made up of energy or power like the sun. All we were doing is focusing it and making it stronger. You have this ability as does Baby and I guess all animals. If you like, I will be happy to teach you what I know," he said as his finger touched the spot between her eyes.

He then showed her how to move objects and bring them to him or send them away. Twice a day they practiced this exercise and twice a day worked in weapons training. Between these times, was spent in study where Don was the teacher. On the ships, they found more than enough books, paper, pens and pencils so it was like having a floating classroom. As the winds continued to increase, the ship's course was diverted to the harbor of Havana.

Chapter 6

During the night as the storm continued to build in momentum, the ship fully automated was diverted and made its way to the harbor of the former capital city of the island of Cuba. Don had been awake for several hours and when the child came on deck he reached for her holding her in his arms while planting a kiss on her forehead. The winds were kicking up and the vessel was rocking but nothing like it had been when they were in the open seas the night before.

"Father, are we safe?" she asked still holding onto him for security.

"I'm sure we are. This is supposed to be one of the most secure harbors in the Caribbean from what I hear," he replied.

"This is Cuba, right?" she asked again. "America and these people used to be enemies, weren't they?"

"Yes, long ago but now, I wonder if anyone survives. We will soon find out. I haven't spotted any fires or any movement so far but best to be cautious. Kind of odd but I do see some lights on in at least one or two buildings. We could dock at the pier but I am thinking as a safety measure to stay where we are until we find out if any people made it. If not, we will stay in that large hotel over there and wait out the storm. We might spend the entire season there if need be."

John H. Cary

After a nice breakfast, they were in the zodiac, the three of them heading the short distance to the shore where they secured the craft and began walking down the main street. Annie had been given a small sword of her own and felt comfortable with it whereas Don was armed to the teeth and Baby had the weapons she always carried. It must have been quite a sight seeing a heavy-armed man in military fatigues accompanied by a half-naked female child wearing only a large t shirt and adult puma walking down an empty street in broad daylight in Havana, Cuba. Cars were scattered abandoned along with the numerous skeletal remains of a once thriving city. Over the course of several months, they had grown used to these and accepted them while feeling fortunate that they were part of the living, maybe the only living. The child was wearing shoes so she wasn't completely nude but she was a child nonetheless and the shirt was just mostly as protection against the heavy winds.

As they approached the hotel which was also a casino, there did appear to be lights on inside. Only then did Don realize that there had been a movement for what was known or to be known as places "going green." Looking up, he saw the masses of solar cells and windmills on the roofs of all buildings in the area and this meant that even if all humanity was dead, there was still power. With Cuba for the most part being assaulted annually by hurricanes, the buildings were limited in height so this particular one was only three floors or stories yet did have a good sprawl to it.

Entering, the first thing they had to do was make sure that there were no people hiding that might create problems. That's where Baby came into play mostly because of her heightened senses. She was instructed to go room to room and either see or smell for human life as Don did the same with the girl acting as his shadow. The child had removed the shirt and shoes which made her feel more comfortable while her human companion looked the part of a soldier. It took several hours but all they could find were the skeletal remains of a lot of people. Deaths must have occurred long ago because there wasn't even the hint of the smell of decomposition. With the storm beginning to rage outside, they had just made it and knew the ship would be safe as it was anchored in a secure spot in the harbor. There was one large room filled with slot machines to amuse them as well as another place called a "V.I.P. Lounge" that had plenty of room to spread out and sleep. He had brought more than enough food for the trio yet Baby had other ideas in mind. With the people gone, some of the animals decided to make this their homes and the cat went hunting. After a few minutes she returned with a large rat in her mouth which she devoured quickly followed by another and another until she had eaten nearly a dozen before belching and collapsing on a large sofa soon falling into a deep sleep. There was plenty of money lying about so Don decided to teach the child about gambling with the machines. As they played, it was a learning experience for the child teaching about math and also history and what money used to mean in both the good and bad ways.

"How do you know all of these things, Father?" she asked.

"I used to own places like this before," he said explaining parts of his previous life. Eventually he might tell her about when he was president but perhaps as she read more books, she would find out on her own. For now all they could do was live in the moment.

A little more than a week passed and soon the storm subsided so they could travel once again. Instead of leaving, they decided to stick around for another week and were happy that they did because as they were about to weight anchor, another storm began brewing. During the time in the hotel and casino, the girl learned not only about money but developed her skills with weaponry. With plenty of rats in the place, she learned about the use of the bow and by the time they decided to leave had become a lethal instrument in the art of killing while also learning how to skin and prepare these animals for meals. Naturally, she enjoyed playing the slot machines especially since she and Don had an unlimited amount of money at their disposal so it didn't matter if they won or lost but actually, between the two of them became very wealthy. He did wonder what it would have been like and the reactions of the customers if there was a heavily armed man, large cat and naked female child in a casino playing slot machines.

"Probably won't allow pets," he thought with a chuckle.

Since the child really had not experienced much of a childhood, all efforts were made for her to play and have fun. She was told she could do anything she wanted to. If she wanted to run around with the cat she could or shoot rats or gamble, it was alright but she did learn rules.

"If you are going outside, I need to know," Don said. "If you are hungry let me know or if you are tired but also we have to have a certain time to study."

Annie was an obedient child and understood what she was told and Don made it a point to let her know why she had to follow those rules and they were for her safety. He wasn't sure if there were others, other people out there that might want to hurt her or perhaps other cats that were not friendly like Baby who might want to eat her.

"A cat would eat me?" she questioned.

"Yes, like I would," he growled and began to blow on her belly tickling her making her laugh.

The girl liked to be touched and played with but it was in an innocent way unlike the first man he had killed named Duncan

Tess who had raped and killed dozens of young girls and boys in the most brutal of ways. Don was happy that people like those no longer existed or he hoped they weren't but could never be sure. He also knew that he had to make sure she was protected in such an uncertain world. It was possible that the two of them were the only ones left in the world and this was troubling because either she would be responsible for re-population of the planet or after one of them died, the race and the species would soon be extinct. It would be a population of animals. Things like this he felt best not to consider. For now they had to wait out the storm and she had to have a childhood.

Finally, after nearly a month, they made the decision to leave and head up the eastern side of the Florida peninsula frequently stopping along the way where they encountered numerous animals including some related to Baby. During stop, she went off and did not return until the following morning and they just assumed she had gone off hunting. She had been making strange howling sounds for nearly a week but Don and Annie simply felt it was growing pains and left it at that.

Chapter 7

Don knew that he had to find out what his legacy was and how he was being remembered or if he was being remembered at all. Were there any people left on the planet besides him and the child? He was happy for her companionship and realized through her that he had never really had a childhood of his own. His father had spoiled him and had trained him since his earliest recollections to be a ruthless individual always seeking control over others and to always win even when he lost. When he did lose, he didn't.

"You cheated!" he would shout or, "we have to do this over because I wasn't ready."

As he reflected on his past, it saddened him and the fact that he didn't do enough to control the pandemic that had not only wiped out his country but the world for all he could tell. Internet was pretty well nonexistent. There had not been any new news for at least a year but fortunately it was running which meant he had a virtual library at his disposal to teach him and the child whatever they wished to learn. Naturally, as he traveled, he went into libraries and took books he felt he might need and now with the young girl, Annie, he had to see to her education. The main thing was her survival which meant training.

Continuing up the coast with land always within sight, they did make numerous stops along the way. He had noticed that his furry companion had begun to gain weight and soon it was easy to determine that she was expecting a litter of cubs. This excited the child knowing that within a couple of months there would be more in the family. Pumas typically have two to four in a litter unlike often twice that number with the smaller domesticated cats which would make caring for them easier. It was good that Don spoke the language and told the large feline that she should begin to find a comfortable place to deliver and care for her young and to let him and Annie know if she needed any help and also when to stay away thus avoiding any potential conflicts or misunderstandings. They felt that perhaps it might be best to have a land base for the event and Don knew of several places in the White House that would be ideal. He just hoped it had survived even if the people had not. Vaccines had been developed and distributed but the virus continued to mutate to the point at which any cure or prevention was generally a waste of time. Most only extended life before the inevitable occurred.

With favorable winds, they were able to make the journey from the tip of Florida to the nation's capital in less than a month. It was then that Don began to spot familiar landmarks which he had not seen in what was in his mind more than four years but in actuality were was some two decades. Annie, however could not remember where she was born or very few memories of her time except for being on the ship and then the island and even had a hard time remembering her parents. Don, however had taken the great foresight to carry along the sealed photo of them that he had found in the submerged wreckage. He didn't want her to forget.

For several days prior to landing at their final destination, they had prepared. During several scavenging trips aboard various vessels, the man was able to find thicker clothes that fit the child plus some excellent boots and even military-style backpacks that fit her small frame. He was lucky to have come across pants that resembled his with many pockets for carrying all kinds of gear. She loved how these looked on her mostly because they appeared similar. The girl had gotten quite skilled with the bow, sword and knife so he knew she could easily handle herself in a difficult situation. He had considered teaching her how to use the handgun but felt it best to instruct her in the use of a small caliber rifle that was within the formerly hidden compartments of the ship. It was light and easy to use and he found twenty, ten round magazines for it and dozens of cases of hollow point .22 ammunition. Along the way, she became a near expert with the weapon which was chosen due to its zero recoil and ease of firing. There were always targets to practice on ranging from limbs of trees to floating debris to small animals. This gave her confidence and also it made him feel like she could have another advantage in the event that there were people remaining or wild animals.

When the navigation system announced their destination was ahead, they were ready. There was a small pier or wharf where they secured the ship and soon they were on their way. It took about half a day to walk to the edge of the city but still had a way to go so they found a small two-story home that actually had doors on it and no human remains where they opted to spend the night. Then in the morning bright and early they made their way to what was once the seat of power.

The girl had seen some books with lots of pictures showing the monuments in Washington, D.C. and when she saw them first-hand was surprised at the size. There were lots of animals about but none who appeared dangerous aside from the occasional stray dog which ran away quickly upon seeing the trio especially the large cat who was becoming more and more uncomfortable.

"Not long Baby. Soon we will be where we can stay for a while and you can become a mother," Don assured the large feline while Annie stroked the spot she liked so well behind her ears causing a loud series of purrs.

By midday they had arrived at what used to be Don's home, the White House. It was easy to enter or easier than it had been in the past. Remains of guards still at their posts fingers on the triggers of unused weapons lay vigilant as reminders of loyalty to the very end. Aside from remains, there were no life forms of any sort that is human life forms although others such as rodents, birds and others began scurrying to their homes within the furniture, walls and ceilings but none were of any threat. Annie did get some practice with the rifle and since Baby was a bit sluggish due to her advanced pregnancy and fattened belly, mostly rats were given to her which she took with gratitude. Don felt that the safest place would his former office known as the Oval Office which also had other more private rooms where the cat could have her privacy to deliver her brood. Like how it was in Havana, many buildings in Washington had become green as they had solar and wind devices to maintain constant power so they always had lights and heat when necessary.

After settling in, the humans decided to explore, although this place was quite familiar to the man. He wondered what busts, portraits or other icons or images remained if any. As they ventured into place that apparently had been set aside for tourists and had to be something akin to a hall of presidents it surprised him that he was memorialized in many ways as he and his former wife plus at least one statue none really displaying him in a negative light.

About that time, Annie who had been looking at the other presidents approached him.

"You were president of the United States, weren't you Father?" she spoke with a smile.

"How'd you know? Couldn't have been due to these portraits."

"I saw you in a book months ago. Were you a bad one?"

"Yes, I believe I was. It was a time when I was still a child on the inside and I feel I will never pay back my sins," he said as tears began to stream down his cheeks.

"Father, maybe you were a bad man before but that was then and this is now. I love you and so does Baby so that's all that matters," she said giving him a hug.

"And I love you, Annie. Thanks."

"They sent you to Alcatraz I read sort of like what they did to Napoleon yet it seems that putting you there was a good thing, wasn't it?"

"Yes, Honey because it allowed me time to think and I needed to have been banished."

Don felt he had been forgiven at least in the eyes of the child but how history viewed him was hard to know.

After few days, Baby in a very silent way presented the family with a family of her own. There was a total of two, a boy and girl both healthy and hungry who cried like any other newborn kittens. It was nice being in a comfortable place yet they had to continue exploring with the hope of finding other survivors of the pandemic.

For several years they remained in the nation's capital but realized it was time to move on. They had continued to train yet also studied and even set up residence in the Library of Congress. Their energy work moving objects was a daily practice yet at times Don realized it worked better with him than with the others. As he watched the girl grow, he realized that time did not pass for him as it did with her and even the cats. He had considered going to a larger city but then felt it would be best to go to the smaller ones more inland or to more isolated locations where perhaps the pandemic had not found some of the more remote locations.

Alcatraz Awaits: The Legacy of Donald Trump

Annie was growing and Baby's children had decided to stay with the group. The only means of travel was mostly by foot yet they were fortunate that the highways were still intact. Internet had been down for the past year with not even automated sites functioning so they had no idea where they were going except west. They had been fortunate that about six months before their departure, they had come across two young mules that were friendly even to the cats who knew not to bother them so they were able to load a wagon with more than enough supplies including extra wheels from cars, food, ammo, bows and arrows and extra clothes mainly for the girl who was still growing plus shoes and boots. They had water purifiers which they had found in the armory so that was not a problem and the cats were capable of hunting as were the humans.

It was springtime and despite lack of maintenance, the cherry trees were in full bloom. At first they all loaded into the wagon but then felt it best to reduce the load so for the most part, they walked. Sometimes when one grew tired, they had a space to sleep. Don got to where he never seemed to grow tired but never let on to this.

Time continued to pass. Days becoming weeks, weeks becoming months, months becoming years, years becoming decades going place to place, town to town never finding another living soul. In his mind, Annie was always a child and he was always her father and never once did he even consider having sex with her as in his mind he always thought that they would find someone, some living human male to become her husband and begin to rebuild the human race. Baby and the cubs along with generations continued to come and go and finally they realized that they were the only ones left. Don also began to finally realize that Annie had one day become an old woman yet he was the same. Her energy was depleting and often they had to stop for longer periods of time to rest. Even with the energy work, they practiced, it could not stop her aging.

One night as they were resting in a place of rolling hills and brutal winters the no longer young girl began to whisper and said, "Father, it's just us, isn't it?"

Then before he could reply, her eyes closed never to open again. There was a large mountain where the images of four former leaders had been carved in stone and that was where she was placed and rest for eternity. With that Donald J. Trump realized that being alone was his legacy.

Chapter 8

It's hard to tell of the passage of time. If you live in an area where there are separate seasons, it's not that hard but in tropical ones nearly impossible. With Donald Trump wandering around even traveling to other countries and continents he continued to search for those who had survived the pandemic, a plague that he was for the most part responsible for allowing to spread.

More than a thousand years passed and an interplanetary spaceship approached the planet.

"Assuming standard orbit, Commander."

"Good job Ensign. Scan for life signs."

"Low forms only except...wait a minute. I am detecting one single advanced life form. Appears to be human. I thought that race had been wiped out."

"Okay, send a probe. Collect samples and images. Maybe we can rebuild the human population on another planet. Don't harm the original. Then document this in our logs and move on."

Donald Trump never felt the samples being taken and continued to wander. How long he continued to live is anyone's guess but having been a self-centered leader, perhaps this was to be his legacy a legacy of being alone, the Legacy of Donald J. Trump.

THE AUTHOR

John H. Cary is a multi-faceted individual with numerous degrees in a wide variety of fields including horticulture, environmental design, political science and Chinese medicine. He hails from a small town in Georgia just south of Atlanta yet for twenty years traveled the globe teaching primarily in Asia. His books include DIXIE WORLD: The Adventures of an Immortal Being (also available in Chinese), SCARY TERRY (available in Chinese), ENEMY FAMILY, WAITING FOR DEATH: Forgotten Stones..., and a host of others with more to come. He is single and interests include weight training, archery and sport fishing.

Review Requested:

We'd like to know if you enjoyed the book. Please consider leaving a review on the platform from which you purchased the book.

Milton Keynes UK
Ingram Content Group UK Ltd.
UKHW020836200524
442968UK00005B/683